HER AMBER CHALICE

A GUARDIANS OF CAMELOT PORTAL FANTASY NOVEL

SARAH BIGLOW

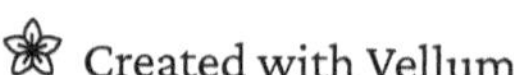 Created with Vellum

FROM THE AUTHOR

Special Thanks to:
Jeffrey.Tristan.Thyme, Monica Leonelle, Adriana Anger, Scott Casey, Ryan James, Vicki Hsu, Molly Zenk, Lorenzo, Michael W. Kerr, Melissa Showers, Gerald P. McDaniel, Finley Ymir, Melanie B., Sara Vath, Niels Starfari, Stephen Ballentine and Kaytea Grounds.

Five days felt like an eternity to wait to announce I was the rightful heir to Camelot. Yet, the tournament had concluded a week ago, I'd been named its victor, and Arthur had been arrested as a spy. He now sat in prison while awaiting trial in Camelot's court system. We'd gotten confirmation that I was in fact Queen Ingrid's biological daughter yesterday, but there were still no plans to make it public knowledge. The strange feeling of loneliness that had hit me after the tournament's conclusion continued to ebb and flow. Most of the week I'd lacked the focus to try and figure out the cause. At least today wasn't so bad.

I stood in front of a mirror in the room I'd been given in the castle. It was three times the size of the one I'd used while staying with Emerys in her cabin. In fact, it was larger than the entire flat I'd shared with Aunt Nim back in London. Not that I was complaining, but part of me didn't know what to do with all the extra space around me.

The process of moving in had been quick and painless. Just one of the many perks of having staff to handle it all for you. I also hadn't packed much in the way of belongings when Emerys and I had fled London the night of Nim's murder. There wasn't time. Thinking about the woman who'd raised me brought tears to my eyes. I brushed the wayward drops that managed to slip down my cheeks away with my right hand. My left arm still remained bandaged and bound against my side in a sling. Compound fractures were a real bitch even in Camelot. Still, magic was pretty amazing, and the doctors had assured me I'd only need the sling for another day or two before I could use my arm without restrictions.

A soft knock on the door interrupted my brooding. I straightened my shirt and closed the distance to the door. I pulled it open to reveal a young woman in the royal family's purple staff uniform on the other side of the threshold.

"Good morning," she greeted, her gaze focused on a point just beyond my left shoulder.

"Uh, morning," I greeted, trying to remember if we'd crossed paths in the last few days.

"I've come to help get you ready. You have breakfast with her majesty," the woman explained, still standing on the other side of the threshold and not making eye contact.

"Help me ... oh. Uh, right. Come on in."

I'd spent so much of my life doing everything for myself. It felt foreign to have people whose sole job was to assist me in whatever I needed, be it getting dressed or fetching me a snack from the kitchen at midnight, because I couldn't sleep.

"Remind me of your name again," I said as she entered and I sat on the edge of the bed, tugging on a pair of ankle high boots with one hand.

"Laverne," she answered and positioned herself behind me, a comb and hair clips appearing from the depths of her pockets.

"Right, Laverne. Sorry, we met the other day," I mumbled, feeling like an idiot.

"You've met a lot of people," she said, easily dismissing it as she tamed my hair into a neat twist at the nape of my neck.

"I promise you won't be doing my hair for long," I said as I stood.

"It's no trouble. Besides, it's my job."

"I know. Fuck … sorry, I'm just not used to all this pampering and primping. I'm not …" I trailed off. I was about to say I wasn't a princess, but that wasn't strictly true.

I *was* a princess by birth and blood. I just hadn't been raised as one. I wasn't sure I'd ever get used to the idea. Maybe the queen keeping our connection tight-lipped for now wasn't such a bad thing. I didn't think I could handle all the extra bowing and people falling over themselves all because I suddenly had a title.

Laverne nodded wordlessly to my partial thought as she helped adjust the sling. "Right. I shall take you to the dining room now if you like."

I appreciated that she didn't assume I knew my way around the palace yet. Besides, as she'd pointed out, escorting me was part of her job too. "Lead on."

I tried my best to commit the route to memory as I followed her down a flight of stairs and a long corridor lined with paintings. All of the portraits I had to assume were my ancestors. We stopped at a set of double doors that opened inward. Laverne gave them a solid shove to throw them wide, revealing the queen sitting at the head of the table. She wore a tunic, similar to the one Emerys had worn the day we'd met, over a pair of looser fitting pants. Her hair was done up in a knot at the top of her head.

She looked up at my arrival and smiled. "Good morning, Morgan. Glad you found us."

Before I could ask who 'us' was, I spotted two familiar faces seated on the other side of the table. Gethin was already on his feet and ushering me over to sit down before I could greet him.

"You wouldn't believe the kitchens they've got here. Industrial everything. I mean, I know it's a castle and they're royalty ... well you're royalty, but if I could cook even just one meal in there, I think I'd die happy," he rambled.

"Morning to you, too, mate," I said as he poured me a cup of coffee from a carafe sitting at the center of the table.

"Gethin is rather star struck," Emerys said from the seat to his right. She'd discarded the dramatic cloaks and sported a short-sleeved navy tunic over a pair of black leggings. She'd pulled her hair into a twist at the nape of her neck. I had to admit, she looked the most relaxed I'd ever seen her.

"You can't blame Gethin for being excited. He's

been dreaming of this ever since he started apprenticing with you," I answered.

Across the table, my mother's face clouded with sadness. All of this was just as new to her as the rest of us. Where I'd grown up wondering what my mother was like, she'd spent the last thirty years not realizing she was missing out on my life. She didn't even know I existed.

"So, you are a practitioner of hearth magic?" she addressed Gethin directly.

"Ah, yes ... I mean, I dabble," he answered, averting his gaze.

"He's being modest. I swear he could make beans on toast into something gourmet," I said.

"Then please have free reign of the kitchens this evening. Whatever ingredients you need, just ask and the staff will provide it. Make your dream meal," she said.

The knife and fork fell from Gethin's fingers clattering against his plate. "You're serious?"

"Quite."

"Thank you, your Majesty." He looked at me and mouthed, 'is this really happening?'

I gave him a smile and a gentle pat on the arm. He collected himself a few moments later and stood.

"I'd better get to work then. Your majesties, Emerys …"

He exited the dining room, leaving me sitting alone with Emerys and my mother. It felt strange to think of the queen in those terms. We'd had a few conversations over the last week, but nothing that shifted our relationship away from being strangers. Still, thinking of her as my mother instead of simply the queen was a deliberate conscious decision on my part to try and remedy that.

Silence fell over the room in Gethin's absence, and I turned my attention to the food on my plate. Eating one-handed was still a skill I hadn't quite mastered. When a raspberry rolled off my plate after my fourth failed attempt to stab it, I let out a groan of frustration. "I swear I'm not usually this clumsy."

My mother gave me a genuine smile. "You really think I'm going to fault you for your table manners when you're recovering from an injury?"

"Honestly, I wouldn't know." I set my fork down on the table. "I know the test proved that I'm your daughter, but it still feels strange. We don't really know each other."

Sadness darkened her features for a moment. "You're right, we don't. And I fear some of that is my own doing. Finding out I have a daughter who was taken from me at birth isn't something I'm going to get over in a week."

"I don't expect you to either. You had this whole other life with an imposter you thought was your child. I get the hesitation. I just wonder if maybe telling everyone else the truth might help? You wouldn't be shouldering this big secret alone."

My mother turned to Emerys, who had up until now remained silent in the discussion. "What do you think?"

"I believe sharing the truth is the right course of action. I understand your trepidation. But the longer this goes unaddressed, the more time our enemies have to use the situation to their advantage."

I hadn't even considered the political shitstorm brewing with Arthur sitting in a cell. There was no denying his fae nature now. But there were still so many unanswered questions, like who'd put the plan in motion to begin with? I knew from what Emerys had told me that the Seelie King was most likely involved to some degree, but was my mother aware? And now that Arthur had been exposed, what happened next?

"Perhaps my fear is less about others knowing the truth of Morgan's lineage and more that I fear losing the support of the people. I was duped for three decades. Even I question my own ability to lead our kingdom. Surely there will be those who'd agree," my mother admitted.

I wanted to tell her that magic could be extremely powerful and in the wrong hands, down-right malicious. But my gut told me she didn't want excuses to justify her feelings.

"The Pendragon line has weathered plenty of storms. This one's yet another we will get through," Emerys said, her tone firm.

My mother reached across the table and took Emerys by the hand. "Can you ever forgive me for cutting you out of my life for so long?"

A breath hitched in Emerys' throat before she answered. "I do not begrudge your actions. I just wish we could have found Morgan sooner. Perhaps then we would find ourselves in a different place."

"Okay ... So, assuming we aren't going to announce that I'm a princess, what's on the agenda today?" I interjected.

"I was hoping you would like to spend the day together," my mother answered.

"I'd like that."

Before anyone else could speak the dining room doors burst open and a young man wearing a secu-rity uniform rushed in. He cast Emerys and I a wary glance before bending to whisper in my mother's ear. I watched her expression shift from a pleasant smile to a drawn face with worry lines creasing her eyes and around her mouth.

"What is it?" Emerys was the first to speak.

"It appears we have a leak in our security. Someone outside of the castle staff has learned the truth about Morgan and they're threatening to publish the information."

If someone else broke the news before the royal family had the chance to, that would definitely undermine my mother's authority as Queen. "Guess we're not having a chill mother-daughter bonding day then," I said.

"It would appear not."

IT TOOK LESS than an hour to pull together the necessary staff to arrange a broadcast from the castle courtyard. I did my best to stay out of the way as workers sorted out the logistics of where we'd each stand during the announcement. A few hand-picked journalists had been summoned and permitted on the grounds. From just inside the doors that led to the courtyard, I watched staff set up what looked like cameras. Only they weren't nearly as high-tech as I'd expected. Just another difference between this world and the one I'd left behind.

An intense wave of longing crashed over me when I caught sight of the stone still situated in the center of the courtyard. Excalibur no longer protruded from within the rock.

Wait. Excalibur.

The blade had called to me during the whole bloody tournament and once I'd freed it from its stony sheath, I'd barely been able to relinquish my grip on it. My mother had taken custody of the sword—keeping it in the throne room, mounted on the wall. I thought back to the times when the loneliness had receded most. She and I had chatted a bit in the throne room, and it was definitely during those times I'd felt the least alone. In the back of my mind, I'd assumed it was because I was finally connecting with someone of whom I shared blood. But what if the sword was still calling to me?

I resolved to ask Emerys about it once the whole media circus was over and the kingdom—and presumably the other races in the realm—knew my true identity. Speaking of Emerys, she was approaching me from across the courtyard.

"I know you have been hesitant to take on the mantle of the Pendragon bloodline, but it would appear you now have no choice," she said.

"I haven't had a choice in any of this—" I reminded her as an aide waved me over, cutting the conversation short.

One of the other personnel applied my makeup to get me camera ready. I turned to see my mother walking out with Excalibur in a leather scabbard attached to a belt. She stopped beside me and held out the weapon.

Relief washed over me at the close proximity to the blade. "You want me to wear it?"

"It is your birthright," she answered and fastened it around my hips for me. The scabbard fell against my left leg, ready to be drawn with my dominant hand.

"We're ready, Your Majesty," one of the blokes who'd been fiddling with the camera called.

My mother squared her shoulders and led the way to the courtyard to address the crowd. I followed her, standing on the spot they'd marked for me earlier. I watched my mother look dead into the lens across the courtyard before she began speaking.

"Citizens of Camelot, I know that there have been many questions in the wake of the annual tournament's revelations. We are diligently investigating how an infiltrator could have gained access to the castle."

She took a breath to compose herself. I had no idea what came next since I wasn't privy to writing the speech.

"There is one question I do wish to answer today. Testing has been conducted and we have confirmed that the man who went by Arthur Pendragon is in fact Seelie. He bears no familial connection to the crown. I speak to you now as a mother. I cannot express in words the grief I have felt at the betrayal of someone I had thought of as my own flesh and blood. But there is a light at the end of this darkness."

She turned to me and placed a hand on my shoulder. "We have also learned definitively that Morgan le Fey is the rightful heir to Camelot. From this day forward she will be known by her birth name, Morgan Pendragon."

TWO

I tuned out the barrage of questions the journalists shouted at my mother. There was no way I would provide any answers. I just stood stoically beside her while she spoke. Eventually, I felt a hand on my shoulder, and it was enough to shake me out of my daze.

Emerys guided me back inside and I slumped against the polished stone wall behind me, letting it keep me upright. "Please tell me this all gets easier?"

"I wish it did. But I am afraid this is only the beginning. Now that everyone knows the truth, your anonymity evaporates. It will not be safe for you to venture beyond the castle walls unguarded."

"Seriously?" I groaned.

"Need I remind you that we originally met

thanks to two highly trained soldiers attempting to murder you?"

"No," I grumbled, wanting to point out that I'd been at a disadvantage that night. My magic had been repressed for decades. Thank goodness it's better now.

The front doors slammed shut, diminishing the ambient light in the entry hall. I looked at my mother. She wiped her eyes before straightening her tunic and joining me as I leaned against the wall.

"I am thankful that task is over with," she sighed.

"I know it's still morning, but I could make you a drink. I'm a bartender by trade," I offered.

"I don't usually condone day drinking, but I think this may be the exception."

She waved me down the corridor and I followed a half step behind her. In my peripheral vision I spotted four guards flanking us, as if they feared something might jump out and attack us at any moment.

Given the fact a Seelie had been living under their noses for so long, part of me couldn't blame them for their hypervigilance. I expected Emerys to join us, but she'd disappeared the moment my mother came inside. We wound our way along a set of corridors I'd not been down yet, dispelling the illusion that I knew where anything was in this place. Somehow, we ended up at my mother's private quarters.

One of the guards stepped up to open the door, putting himself between her and the interior of the room. We waited until he gave the all clear before entering. I'd expected something old-fashioned with antique chairs and a fireplace. Her quarters boasted plush lounge chairs in several hues of forest green and surprisingly no hint of a fireplace. However, I did spot ducts in the ceiling pumping in cool air. I spotted the bar along the far wall. Or rather a counter built into the wall with a few bottles displayed and some empty glasses.

I pivoted to ask what she wanted when I felt the hilt of the sword bump against my leg. I reached across my torso to try and unfasten the belt with my good arm, but had the wrong angle. "You probably want this back."

She held up a hand. "As I said, it is your birthright. Excalibur belongs with you now."

"Do people really go around just sporting ceremonial weapons here?" I knew the palace guards at Buckingham did, but none of them carried a mystical blade.

"Goodness, no. I just meant, you don't have to give it back. Honestly, I believe it is safer in your possession than sitting in the throne room on display."

"It's going to sound crazy, but I think it wanted to be near me, too. Not that a sword has thoughts or emotions … but when I wasn't near it, I had this sort of longing I couldn't quite explain. I think I was missing Excalibur."

"I've felt that, too. But not in a very long time. I remember it from right after it was passed to me by my mother."

I stopped fiddling with the belt and pointed to the shelf. "What do you fancy?"

"I'm afraid I'm not very adventurous when it comes to my alcohol consumption," my mother noted. "I do enjoy a good Scotch now and again."

A strangled sound caught in my throat at the mention of Nim's favorite drink. "Scotch it is," I finally croaked out as I grabbed the bottle and two glasses. I poured some of the clear liquid into each glass and passed one over. I settled into one of the plush chairs as best I could with a sword strapped to my hip. We toasted and tossed back the contents. I still couldn't help grimacing at the taste.

"I take it this is not something you inherited," she said with a laugh.

"Nope." After a moment, I added, "It was my Aunt Nim's favorite, too."

"I remember her only in bits and pieces. If I'm honest, a lot of the day you were born is a blur."

"I've heard labor can be draining," I said.

"I'd lost your father not long before you were born. At the time, I'd convinced myself the hazy feeling was just grief playing with my emotions. But I now believe magic was at play even then. I know that there were complications when you were born. I remember them telling me I'd lost a lot of blood."

"Well, Nim might have been Seelie-born, but she only ever told me happy stories about Camelot. I think she wanted me to know that I had a place waiting for me. I don't know, maybe she felt guilty for taking me from you."

"I am grateful she took such good care of you." She made a gesture for me to pour her another glass.

I obliged. "You know she was murdered by Seelie soldiers," I declared, my tone softening.

"You're certain?"

I tapped the tip of my ear. "The pointy ears are kind of hard to forget. If Emerys hadn't found me when she did, we wouldn't be having this conversation."

"It may not have occurred on our soil, but an attack on the royal family cannot go ignored."

"What will you do?"

"I have some covert military assets I can deploy to do some digging and see what they can find out."

"Any progress in getting anything out of Arthur?" I hated saying his name or even thinking about him. My arm throbbed from just the memory of what he'd done.

She hesitated, taking another sip of scotch before answering. "I know it is my duty to get to the bottom of what happened ... but I look at him and still see the little boy who I sang to sleep at night. The young man who showed such kindness to those less fortunate."

"You can't reconcile the boy you knew with the man who nearly killed me to take the crown."

"No. And he knows our tactics. He had insisted on training with our investigators to understand their methods. He's not saying anything."

That seemed a calculated maneuver in case he ever did get caught. "I could take a crack at him."

"While that might give you some closure, I don't think it is a good idea."

"Do we know who he actually is? I mean, you've got to wonder who set all of this in motion."

"King Uther is manipulative and has held his throne for longer than I've held mine. But I can't really believe he'd put something like this in motion."

"From what Emerys told me, she thinks he's behind it. But even if that's the case, where'd Arthur come from?"

"I doubt he knows himself," she answered, draining the rest of the liquid from her glass. "I didn't mean to make this about all of our troubles. I truly wanted to get to know you."

"I'm an open book," I replied.

"Part of me doesn't know what to ask," she admitted.

"Well, I grew up in a two-bedroom flat in London. Magic was an open secret where I grew up. Which had its upsides. I could go around saying I was a witch, and no one batted an eye. But ask me to prove it, and that's where things got complicated."

"I saw you perform extraordinary magic during the tournament."

"If you'd met me a week earlier, you'd think you were seeing a completely different person. Nothing I did ever went right. Turns out it was because I couldn't connect to the magic in the world around me."

"Well, something tells me that isn't going to be a problem from now on."

"Doesn't appear that way," I replied.

She held up her empty glass and asked, "What made you go into this line of work?"

"Desperation, mostly. I guess I was never the best in school and this was something I could do without magic while still being close to it."

"I'm sorry you had to go through those experiences."

I shrugged. "I'm not. They made me who I am. And to be honest, I like who I am."

She nodded, turning the glass over in her hands. "Is there anyone romantic in your life?"

I snorted. "No. I mean I've dated plenty, but nothing serious." Taron's naked form flashed in my memory, and I busied myself with pouring another drink. Maybe she'd think the flush in my cheeks was a byproduct of the alcohol.

"Well, there are plenty of eligible bachelors ... or bachelorettes in Camelot."

"Noted," I said, downing a second glass of scotch. I set the empty glass down on the tiny table between our chairs. "Can I ask you something?"

"Anything."

"Do you ever wish you were just a normal person? Not born to all this royal stuff?"

She tilted her head to one side in thought. "There was a time when I was a teenager where I resented the responsibilities, I knew would one day be placed on me. But I can't imagine doing anything else now. Eventually I grew into it."

"I still worry I'm not cut out for it. All these people always following you around, doing things for you. It's—"

"Oppressive?" she offered.

"Exactly."

"I promise, once we've sorted everything with Arthur's trial, we can lessen security."

"I hope your justice system moves faster than the one back home."

I caught the look of disappointment in her expression at my words. It took me a second to realize what had caused her reaction. I still thought of London as home.

"I'm sorry, it's all just so new," I said, trying to explain myself.

"You don't have to explain or apologize. Camelot isn't your home, not yet. But I hope one day you will come to think of it that way."

I was about to tell her I hoped it would too, but a wave of energy hit me, knocking me sideways off the chair. I landed awkwardly on my bad arm. Tendrils of pain wrapped themselves around my left arm and shoulder. I let out a hiss as a new pain erupted from my hip. I struggled to right myself and looked down to find I'd managed to jam Excalibur's pommel into my side.

"What the fuck was that?" I said, forgetting my audience for a moment.

My mother opened her mouth to answer when a high-pitched keening filled the space, and I could swear the walls around us shook. I did my best to drown out the noise by covering my right ear as we both got to our feet. The door slammed open to my right and Emerys burst inside.

"The cells have been breached," she bellowed.

"What?" I shouted. I'd made out her words, but they lacked meaning.

Emerys waved her hands and the sound around us died down. The door which she'd left open slammed shut and I watched the interior lock click into place. We weren't getting out of here any time soon. I had to admit the sudden quiet was almost painful until my ears readjusted to the noise level.

"There was an explosion," Emerys continued, addressing my mother.

"Has anyone been injured?"

"It's too soon to make that determination. What we do know is the only prisoner being held there is now gone."

"Why do I get the feeling that prisoner was Arthur?" I interjected.

My mother began pacing, wringing her hands. "He was restrained."

"Magically?" I pressed.

"Of course. The moment he was taken into custody."

"Is that standard protocol?"

She nodded.

"You said he had trained on all of that. Could he have figured a way around it?"

"It's possible," she answered.

"More likely, he had accomplices," Emerys noted. "Everyone who witnessed your match during the tournament saw his Seelie nature," Emerys explained. "While we do not yet have confirmation, I suspect he holds a special place in King Uther's inner circle."

"What about people sympathetic here in Camelot? I mean until a week ago, he was the crown prince. Maybe there were protesters who didn't want to see him locked up?" I suggested.

"Either option is dangerous, but accusing a foreign power of a prison break takes us to the brink of war," my mother answered.

"What do we do now?" I doubted hiding out in the queen's private quarters while shit hit the fan was the right move.

Not that I wanted another confrontation with Arthur or anyone who allied themselves with him. Despite that, he also couldn't be allowed to roam free. Not when he had such intimate knowledge of the castle and the inner workings of the royal family.

"We wait for the security team to ensure there is no lingering threat. Then we assess the damage." My mother's tone shifted, detaching emotionally from the situation.

"Well, I'm not going to sit around," I said and shoved past Emerys to unlock the door.

"Morgan, you may have been claimed by the queen, but you are still a stranger to the people in this castle. We cannot afford for you to be swept away in the clean up," Emerys called.

I gestured to the sword on my hip. "Something tells me I'm going to be just fine."

The moment I stepped out of the room, all hell

broke loose around me once more. The wailing of the alarms seemed higher pitched than in the queen's private quarters and the energy wave pulsated on a loop.

"Brilliant move, Morgan," I muttered. "Charging off half-cocked with no fucking idea where to go."

On my hip, Excalibur warmed to the point I feared it would melt through the scabbard and burn me. I managed to free the blade and held the sword in my right hand. The metal glowed blue, illuminating a path ahead of me. Who was I to argue with a magic sword?

Excalibur led me down into the bowels of the castle, through a passage and out into a block of cells. They each housed a bed, sink, and metal toilet. Where the far wall should have been now stood a pile of rubble, dust still billowing in the wind.

Contrary to Emerys' concern, no one stopped me. No one even approached as I made my way to the damaged wall and climbed out. Despite the morning sunlight, the path Excalibur illuminated for me was as visible as if I'd been walking in darkness.

'Hurry!'

The blade appeared to urge me onward in my mind and my feet picked up the pace in response. All around me, the scent of lime hung in the air. It was enough of a signal. My increased speed was thanks to my magic, but I didn't feel the usual effects. There was throbbing headache or nausea I typically experienced when I tried to do a spell.

I had no idea what I expected to find or where the path might lead me. It took me away from the castle grounds into a forested area I'd never encountered before. The magic around me buoyed my feet forward in time to catch a glimpse of Arthur's retreating form, surrounded by several darkly clad figures. They stopped long enough to cross a small stream and Arthur turned back, spotting me.

I wanted to move, to stop him from escaping, but it was as if my magic had rooted me to the spot. I did catch a glimpse of a figure waiting on the other side of the stream—King Uther. He embraced Arthur before they vanished from sight.

CHAPTER
THREE

"Are you certain you saw King Uther?" Emerys demanded when I'd made my way back into the castle with Excalibur's guidance.

"He's kind of hard to forget," I replied.

"It was from a distance. You have to be sure," the Queen said, pacing the length of her private quarters.

"I know what I saw. Arthur had some mercenary looking blokes with him. They crossed a stream and Uther was standing there waiting for them. He gave Arthur a hug and then they just vanished," I recited.

"You were wise not to pursue them," Emerys said.

"Not like I had a choice. It was as if my magic was keeping at a distance. I don't want to say that it wanted him to get away, but ... that's sort of what it felt like."

No, that wasn't quite right. It hadn't been my magic that held me back. I looked down at the sword still clutched in my hand. Excalibur had power all its own and had kept me from running off into a situation I couldn't handle.

"Whatever the reason, I'm glad you're safe," my mother said, pulling me into a one-armed hug. She was careful not to put too much pressure on my injured arm.

A stocky man with close cropped hair and intense green eyes appeared in the doorway. He offered a brief bow before addressing the queen. "Your Highness, the Council has convened. But there is something you should see."

He handed over a phone, a video cued up to play. Emerys and I crowded around her to see as she tapped the center of the screen. Two flags waved in the background behind an obsidian black podium. I could just make out the words at the top of the screen, *Semper virtutis et gloriae.* The Seelie court's motto. Arthur had shouted it at the end of the tournament right before he'd been taken into custody. My chest tightened as King Uther stepped into view.

"Today is a great day for our people," Uther

began in a deep voice. The camera panned to reveal Arthur standing beside him. "Many years ago, the Queen and I welcomed a son, but enemies of our great kingdom abducted and held him against his will. It is with great joy that I welcome our son, Arthur, back where he belongs."

"That's bullshit," I spat. "He's using what happened to me ... what *he* did to me and twisting it."

Uther's address continued. "We will take all appropriate measures to seek justice for the atrocity committed against our family and this kingdom. *Semper virtutis et gloriae.*"

The queen handed the phone back and gave a curt nod. "Let the council know we are on our way."

"What exactly does this council do?" I asked, following her out of her quarters and turning left down an inclined corridor.

"They provide guidance, assist in making new laws."

"So, it's like Parliament," I said, earning me a confused look from both her and Emerys. "Never mind."

The corridor dead-ended at a set of large doors with ornate brass handles that felt out of place with the sapphire and steel aesthetic the rest of the castle boasted. Two guards stepped up to open the doors, allowing the queen to enter. I was hot on her heels when they stepped forward, barring me from entering.

"Oy, I'm with the Queen," I said, trying to push past.

"Only the ruling monarch is permitted," the guard to my right answered in a gruff tone.

I had half a mind to demand whether they knew who I was, but that seemed a good way to get knocked on my arse. I took a step back and Emerys stepped up.

"The Queen has reinstated my status as counselor."

The guard who'd told me off stepped out of her way. I had just enough time to catch a glimpse of a long rectangular table lined with chairs, each filled with people. The queen took up the spot at the head of the table and Emerys moved to sit beside her.

That was all I could glimpse before the guards slammed the doors shut and moved to block all access to the handles. I held up my right hand and shuffled back again. "I get it. I'm not allowed."

I assumed my mother or Emerys would come find me once their emergency meeting wrapped up, so I did my best to find my way back to my room. I ended up two floors down and wandered into the kitchen to find a half dozen different dishes in progress. To my surprise, Gethin was nowhere to be seen. Unease tightened the muscles between my shoulder blades as I left the space to look for my friend. The kitchen wasn't that far from the cells.

"I've been looking all over for you." Gethin's voice rang out and he came into view as I rounded a corner.

"I've been looking for you, too," I replied and offered a brief one-armed hug when he reached me. "Everything's gone to shit."

"I felt the explosion, but I didn't know where you'd gone. No one would tell me. And now I can't find Emerys."

"She's in some emergency convocation of the queen's council. Which, fun fact, even though I'm confirmed royalty, I'm not allowed in."

"That seems like poor leadership training," he muttered. "What has them convening? They aren't usually in session during the summer."

"Have you really not heard?" he gave me a confused look. "Arthur escaped."

"Oh, that is not good."

"And even worse, he's apparently King Uther's son. Which means he's still a prince. And his arsehole father just broadcasted a speech basically accusing the queen of kidnapping his son and threatening war."

His face fell and he pulled off his glasses, rubbing the bridge of his nose. "When Emerys told me she was going to find you, I never thought it would mean something like this."

"And I did? Until two weeks ago, I'd given up on believing any of this was real. And now I'm in the middle of a fucking political incident. I didn't sign up for this."

"The council will figure out what to do. No one but the Seelies would want a war."

"I mean I don't even know who our allies are," I railed.

"I keep forgetting how much you don't know," he said. "I'm not saying that to be mean or anything just ... I have to adjust my own expectations."

"It's fine. If you want to help, give me the run down before they come back, so I don't look like a complete twit."

"Historically, the Seelies have been so brutal that no one wants to align with them. They figure it's easier to band together. We've had alliances with the Unseelie court and the dragons. But no one's heard from the Unseelie court in a long time. And last I heard, the dragons were trying to just keep to themselves."

"So, what you're saying is we're fucked if war does break out?"

"I don't know."

I couldn't blame him for his uncertainty. I was asking him to predict the future and as far as I knew neither of us had that ability. I wasn't sure if anyone did.

"Look, even if everything goes to shit, it's not going to happen tonight, right?"

He looked up at me, putting his glasses back on his nose. "Probably not."

"So, let's try not to go all doom and gloom until we have to."

"Right. Good plan. There will be plenty of time to panic later." He offered a weak smile. "I should get back to cooking. At least I know that's something I can control."

"Mind if I watch the master work?"

That earned me a wider, more confident grin. "Maybe I can teach the princess a few culinary tricks."

"Please don't call me that."

"Why not? It's what you are."

"It still feels like everyone's talking about

someone else when they use words like princess. I'm just me."

"Okay, I promise not to call you princess until you're ready. Now come on, the kitchen awaits."

We wound our way back and I sat on a high stool at a center island while Gethin flitted from dish to dish. He rattled off ingredients and tidbits about sauces and glazes that went in one ear and directly out the other. Still, it was a nice distraction from the drama unravelling elsewhere in the castle.

"Here taste this," he said, shoving a spoon in my face.

I had no idea what it was, but it tasted of honey and sugar with a hint of what I swore was lemon. "Mmm," I offered as I set the spoon down.

"Not too much brown sugar?" He looked worried.

"Tasted perfect to me."

"Okay. Good."

He went back to dicing vegetables and he set another pair of knives to mincing different cuts of meat. Across the way, I spotted what looked like a three-layer cake that was frosting itself. When the world wasn't about to be in peril, I needed to ask him how he managed to keep all of that magic straight. If I'd tried something this complex, we'd end up with diced cake bits and frosted greens.

Time passed as Gethin continued to cook and by the gurgle in my belly, I knew it was at least lunchtime. I hopped off the stool and went rummaging through cabinets until I'd found some cheeses, breads, and what looked like some sort of roasted ham. I slapped together a sandwich and had just bitten into it when low voices filtered through the open door.

I looked up to find Emerys and my mother walking in. Gethin stopped his food preparation and offered a brief bow at the waist. Judging by the fact they weren't flanked by armed guards, I held on to the tiny seed of hope that everything would just blow over.

"What'd they decide?" I broke the silence. Gethin returned to meal prep, but I could tell by the way his head cocked to one side that he wasn't about to miss a word of our conversation.

"We have managed to avoid any declarations of war," Emerys answered.

"No war is good news," I said, taking another bite of sandwich.

"For now, at least. It wasn't easy to keep a lot of the egos restrained. Like you, many of the members took great offense to the suggestion that anyone in our kingdom, let alone the queen would steal a child, or hold them captive for so long," my mother noted.

"You can't tell me you didn't want to reach through the screen and punch that lying piece of shit in the throat," I countered.

"Perhaps over the years I have just learned to keep my emotions in check. Believe me, I am beyond furious by Uther's accusations. I have no doubt it was in response to our announcement this morning."

"So, we may not be sounding the drums of war, but we've got to do something, right? We can't just let him get away with spewing all those lies and threatening us."

"We have an ambassador we will be sending with a security delegation to the Seelie court to discuss a peaceful resolution to the situation," my mother answered.

"You really think they'll talk peace? They seemed pretty damn riled up and looking to pick a fight," I said.

"Uther may be brash, but he knows how it looks, too. At the very least, he will receive our delegation and go through the motions of hosting and engaging in peace talks."

"But we need to be prepared for when those negotiations fail," Emerys added. "I have long suspected that your destiny is far greater than simply returning home to Camelot, Morgan."

I didn't like where she was headed with this. "Look, I'm the last person you want on a delegation. I'm terrible at posh etiquette and I swear like a sailor."

"You aren't going," my mother said. "In fact, as far as anyone outside these walls is concerned, you aren't leaving the castle at all until the situation is resolved one way or another."

"How is that fair?" I argued.

My mother stepped up and put a hand on my good shoulder. "I said as far as anyone outside the castle knows. I am not going to keep you locked up, much as I might want to in order to keep you safe." She glanced back at Emerys. "But she is right, your destiny is beyond these walls."

"What am I supposed to do now? I already pulled the sword from the stone."

"I believe you are meant to be Camelot's greatest defender against our most dangerous enemy," Emerys said cryptically.

"What gave you that idea? A fortune cookie?"

The bewilderment at my unfamiliar turn of phrase flashed in her eyes, but faded in an instant. "Must I remind you that the magic in this world possesses a greater level of sentience than the realm from which you came?" The exasperation in her tone set me on edge.

"Fine, so how exactly am I supposed to be some great defender?"

Emerys looked caught off guard by my question. After a moment of silence, she said, "It is for you to learn. I am merely a supporter on your journey."

"Do you at least have an idea of where I'm meant to start?"

Her face brightened and her eyes twinkled in the overhead light of the kitchen. "That I do. We must return to the Crystal Cave. The answers to your questions lie within its depths."

FOUR

Part of me wanted to laugh at her suggestion that the cave would show me my destiny. But I couldn't argue with the fact it had given me the answers I'd needed to control my magic. I still refused to believe the place was sentient, but I could respect it had some seriously strong power.

"Can't it wait until tomorrow to go?" I protested when Emerys insisted we leave immediately. "Gethin's put in all this work, and it would be a shame to not get to at least try it."

"Destiny kind of trumps dinner," Gethin said, sounding resigned to the fact his efforts were for naught. Almost like his skills being overlooked was a common occurrence.

Way to shoot yourself in the foot, mate.

Emerys looked ready to tell me off when my mother cleared her throat, drawing attention to herself. "I understand the urgency. I do not disagree that setting Morgan on her path is important. But surely, we could wait just a few hours. Let him have this moment."

"We will leave at sundown," Emerys relented.

"Great, we can eat an early supper and be on our way with full bellies," I said.

Emerys turned and it was only then that Gethin gave me an appreciative look and mouthed 'thanks.' My mother gestured to me and made a shooing motion. "I think you ought to get a little rest first. I don't know what awaits you, but more sleep can't be a bad thing."

"You know, this is the first time my mother has actually sent me to my room," I quipped with a smirk.

I retreated to my room and managed to undo the belt holding Excalibur to my hip. I laid it on the floor beside the bed. It wasn't exactly within easy reach, but it also wasn't in a place where someone might make off with it. Next, I settled on the bed, plucking the sling from around my neck and letting my arm fall naturally. It still twinged if I moved it too quickly, but I could feel that the bones had mended.

I wasn't about to lay on it or anything, but it felt nice to not have it pinned to my side. I angled myself against the pillows and pulled my phone off the side table where I'd left it charging. The bit of magic Gethin bought for me the week prior had run its course and given me signal to get through for one call. I'd only been able to leave that one voicemail for Julayne and I hadn't gotten any more texts. I had half a mind to make my way back to the shop and demand a do-over. After all, the shopkeeper wouldn't deny the crown princess, would he?

I hated myself for thinking in those terms. It made me feel spoiled and ridiculously privileged. Despite all of Aunt Nim's stories about Camelot and me being a princess, she hadn't raised a spoiled child. Starting to think of myself in that way dishonored her memory, which only made me feel more like shit. I let out a frustrated groan before shutting my eyes and counting to ten in my head. It was a trick Jules had taught me not long after our first encounter as kids.

I might not be able to call my best friend, but I could still record a message to her. I might never get to send it, but at least I would know I'd tried. So, I opened our text conversation and tapped the microphone icon in the message.

"Hey, Jules, it's me. I don't know if this is going to go through, but I wanted to bring you up to speed." I let out a breath that turned into a hiccup of hysterical laughter. "Where to begin ... well, since the last message I left you, I found out all of Aunt Nim's stories really were true. Well, I suppose she didn't tell me about the absolutely brutal tournament of champions they hold every year. That's one way to scar a kid for life. Anyway, turns out that I can now access my magic, and I'm not half bad at it."

I stretched out my left arm as I continued. "I pulled a fucking sword out of a rock. Like a real actual Excalibur. We're sort of bonded now, I guess. Not exactly how I pictured getting bling. Oh, and I am now recognized as the crown princess of Camelot."

I paused to collect myself. "I still can't quite wrap my head around it all. And it still isn't the same without you here. I'm getting ready to do something ... uh, I don't know what, probably something insane and dangerous. I wish I could tell you more, but I don't have details. Maybe one day I'll come home, and I can tell you all about it over a bourbon. I love you, Jules. Talk soon."

I tapped the microphone again and watched as it

transcribed my message. Out of habit, I hit the send button anyway. Maybe there was some bit of divine magic floating in the air that would feel my deep need to reach my last connection to my past and fulfill that desire. I couldn't bring myself to look down at the screen. Setting my phone aside, I leaned back against the pillow and closed my eyes, allowing myself to drift off into a light doze.

When I woke, the sun had begun its afternoon descent toward the horizon. Grogginess clung to me as I struggled to sit up, letting out a hiss of pain when I tried to push off the bed with my left arm.

"Morgan, you in there?" Gethin's voice came through the closed bedroom door.

For a moment, my grogginess won out and I couldn't remember why he would come looking for me. *Food!* I scrambled out of bed, scooping up the belt with Excalibur, and flung it unceremoniously over my shoulder before opening the door.

"I'm starving," I announced and pushed past him into the corridor.

He fell into step beside me as we made our way down to the dining room where I'd shared breakfast with the queen and Emerys. Gethin was oddly quiet for someone who was about to present a meal to his queen.

"What's going on in that head of yours?" I said, nudging his arm with my elbow. "If you're nervous about the meal, I'm sure it all came out perfectly."

"It's not that. I just can't help thinking … worrying really, that now you're here, Emerys won't have time to continue my training."

"She's a very powerful witch, I'm sure she can handle having two students at once. Besides, sometimes I don't get what she's saying. You're my translator."

"You're probably right, but I just have a feeling that my time is done. And part of me is glad that I'll be able to make my own way in the world. But there's another part of that feels like there's so much more she could teach me."

"Well, you don't have to worry, because I am not letting her get rid of you. You and I are a package deal. You were the first real friend I made here. And I don't take that lightly."

He brightened at my words and adjusted his glasses, hurrying ahead of me a few paces so he could open the door. Emerys and my mother were already seated inside. Dishes heaped with delicious smelling glazed meats and roasted vegetables were laid out along the middle of the table. Gethin pulled out my chair. He beamed at me with such excitement I didn't have the heart to tell him I was capable of pulling out my own chair.

"You might want to remove that," my mother said, gesturing to my shoulder.

My cheeks burned with embarrassment as I realized I'd trekked through the castle with the sword slung over me like a wrestler brandishing their winning belt. I managed to slide it off and set it on the floor without looking too undignified. At least it was only the four of us in the room.

"This all looks wonderful," my mother said, addressing Gethin.

Before Gethin could reply, a soft knock sounded at the door. He darted from his seat and opened it to reveal a young woman in an apron holding two bottles and some glasses. He whispered something to her before she departed and he returned to the table, revealing two bottles of wine—one red, one white.

"We've two courses and the wines pair with each," he explained, popping the cork from the red wine first.

I took a sip after he'd poured everyone a glass and could have melted it was *that* good. This was shaping up to be an excellent meal.

Sneaking out of the castle after three glasses of wine was not the best decision I'd ever made. I might tend bar, but I have never been one to hold my liquor particularly well. And wine made me argumentative as fuck.

"You've got to be quiet and keep the hood up," Emerys chided as she and Gethin ushered me off castle grounds.

"You know, you can't get rid of him," I said, pointing to Gethin as if she hadn't spoken.

"No one is getting rid of anyone, now be quiet," she replied.

"You're kind of mean sometimes. Bet no one's ever had the balls to tell you that."

Emerys tightened her grip on my right arm as she led me in the direction of the highspeed rail line. I heard Gethin rummaging through a bag as we walked. I did not relish the thought of being on a fast-moving train.

"Morgan, drink this." Gethin passed me a small flask. Immediately I tried to hand it back. Didn't he realize plying me with more alcohol was a rubbish idea? Instead, he moved to stand in front of me, unscrewed the top, and foisted it back on me. "Drink."

"Bossy," I grumbled, but took the flask and downed the contents.

It tasted like slightly spoiled orange juice. I fought my gag reflex as a wave of nausea brought me to my knees. My whole body convulsed as it tried to expel the taste. But nothing came up which was strange. A hot flash ripped through my body next, leaving behind a clammy cold sweat.

"What the fuck was that?" I demanded when the feeling passed.

"Hangover cure," he replied and extended a hand to pull me up.

"I hate you right now," I groaned. "But I also kind of love you."

"Now that we've sorted your inebriation, we need to move," Emerys urged.

"Lead on, fearless leader." I gave her a hand flourish with a bow.

I expected to have to sneak through the turnstiles at the station and hop on the last outgoing train. Instead, Emerys steered us away from the entrance altogether. She led us along what looked like a maintenance tunnel that let out beyond the station.

She tugged the hood down over my face as she held up her hand and traced a circle in the air ahead of us. Ozone crackled and made the hairs on the back of my arms stand on end. The forest by the Crystal Cave was just visible through the circle.

"Please tell me I'm hallucinating," I whispered to Gethin.

"Nope, it's real."

Without warning Emerys shoved me through the portal. It widened to accommodate my full height and I staggered forward, catching myself on a tree branch. Emerys and Gethin came through behind me in a more sure-footed fashion and the portal blipped out of existence.

"Have you always been able to do that?" I asked as I turned to face the woman.

She nodded wordlessly.

"Then why did you make me get on a train and a ferry to get to fucking Ireland?"

She tugged a necklace from beneath her tunic top. It was a tiny gold dragon with a diamond at its center. "Portal magic is a borrowed gift. I was not certain it would work in the other realm. And it is not an infinite resource. I must conserve it for times of great need only."

It was a reasonable explanation, but it didn't

mitigate my annoyance. She gestured to the mouth of the cave. I walked inside, retreating to the back where I'd had a strange encounter with its magic about two weeks ago.

The air was sweet, smelling of fresh berries as I settled on a rock and peered down into the shallow pool of water. My reflection looked up at me, wearing the same expression I did.

"Okay, I'm not really sure how this works. But if you know anything about this destiny of mine and how I'm supposed to go about … uh, fulfilling it or whatever, I'd appreciate any hints … please."

The air inside the cave warmed and my reflection in the water rippled, changing to reveal what looked like a grassy field. I could make out myself in the midground with Excalibur held aloft. The scene shifted rapid-fire panning over figures so quick I couldn't make out much beyond general feminine curves. Sunlight beamed down overhead, and an array of colors sparkled around me in the water, blinding me.

I blinked to try and clear my vision. Slowly the image resolved to show me sitting there beside the pool. My vision finally cleared, and I tried to process what I'd seen. I was leading some sort of charge and there appeared to be a lot of women with me.

"Okay, so I'm meant to what … lead an army? Not really the military type here."

"Leaders aren't born, they're made," my reflection told me.

"You clearly haven't met me," I muttered.

My reflection took on a disapproving expression. "You are the Pendragon heir. You are destined for great things, but you cannot do it alone."

"Yeah, I gathered that from the whole cadre of women shown with me there. But what am I meant to do now? We're teetering on the edge of war already and I've been in Albion for less than a month."

The water's surface shimmered, showing what looked like a golden cup. Yet I couldn't make out anything about where it might be or why it was important. Before I could ask for clarification, my reflection returned. She reached up and touched the hollow of her collar bone. As she did so, I felt something pressed against my skin. I looked down to find a necklace with a silver locket resting against my chest.

"This will be your guide."

My reflection flickered, returning to my mirror image looking perplexed. I pulled the locket over my head with my good arm and fiddled with the tiny clasp keeping it closed. The front fell open to reveal a compass, the tiny needle pointing out of the cave. Following it, I emerged and found Emerys and Gethin standing watch. Gethin was first to turn at the sound of my footsteps.

"Where'd that come from?"

"Magic cave," I answered and glanced down at the object in my hand to find the needle had shifted direction. "Hope one of you is good at navigation, because it looks like we're going on a road trip."

CHAPTER
FIVE

I offered the necklace to Emerys. Together we stood there in the forest surrounded by silence as she studied the compass. She held it aloft, turning it over and examining it for what I couldn't begin to guess.

"It just appeared to you?" Gethin asked.

"It's going to sound mental, but I gave it to myself. Well, my reflection in this pool of water did and it showed me a gold cup. Don't ask me what the hell that means, because I've got no idea."

"Maybe you didn't have enough hangover cure," he murmured.

"Morgan was not inebriated. The cave has been known to produce physical manifestations in the past." Her left hand moved absently to brush against the top of her tunic where the golden dragon necklace lay just beneath the fabric. She passed the compass back. "Did it show you anything else?'

I closed my eyes, trying to solidify the flashes of images I'd seen. But the only one that stood out was me leading the charge surrounded by a bunch of women. "The cave told me whatever it is I'm supposed to do, it's not alone. It showed me leading a group of women."

"Most of the military here are men," Gethin offered.

"Would have never guessed," I muttered. "But I have a feeling that whatever we do next it isn't going to be here in Camelot."

I turned the compass over in my hand again, opening it up to look at the needle. It pointed dead ahead of us. But that meant ...

"How far are we from the barrier between this realm and London?"

"Two or three meters at most," Emerys replied.

I pointed ahead of me. "That way?"

"Yes."

"Definitely not staying in Camelot, then. It's leading us...h-home."

Emerys moved to stand beside me, consulting the compass in my palm. "So, it would appear. We

need to prepare for a journey through the Crystalline Gate."

UNLIKE ME, Gethin and Emerys didn't have their belongings readily accessible for travel. We headed back to the cabin first, so they could each pack a bag. I stood in the doorway to Gethin's room and watched him hem and haw over what to bring.

"You're worse than Jules," I said with a laugh. "She'd pack for a weekend trip and bring half her wardrobe."

"I've never been out of Camelot before," he admitted, slumping onto the bed.

"Never?"

He shook his head. "Coming here to study with Emerys was the farthest I'd been. And it's not like she travels much, or at least she didn't before now."

"Well, you're going to be fine. From what I can tell both realms are pretty similar. Just pack for summer weather and you'll be fine."

"Pack nothing you can't fit in a single pack," Emerys called from down the hall.

He still looked nervous as he stared at the pairs

of shorts and pants strewn on the floor. "What if my magic disappears when we pass through?"

His fear wasn't lost on me. I'd been worrying about the same thing since I realized we'd be heading back through the barrier to my realm. I didn't have the answers to quell that fear, but I said, "You've had thirty plus years to hone your skills. It might be a tad harder to connect, but you've got the skills. Besides, you probably won't even need to use magic while we're gone."

He offered a half smile. "I guess I'm about to be the one out of my depth."

"And that's why you've got me to keep your head above water," I said.

I stepped into the room and scooped up a few sets of clothes and shoved them into the over the shoulder pack he'd laid out on the bed beside him. "Come on, something tells me we shouldn't be lingering around here for long."

We reconvened in the small eating area. Emerys had tugged her hair back into a knot at the nape of her neck and carried a similar pack to the one Gethin brought.

"We need to return to the castle and inform the queen about our plans," Emerys said. She pressed her index finger to the necklace at her throat and sketched a circle in the air in front of her. The castle's entryway appeared in front of us.

That answered the question of how we were getting back. It made a certain amount of sense. If no one had seen us leave the castle, it would look suspicious if we came back on the train. Gethin stepped through first and I followed after him. Emerys brought up the rear and the spell snapped shut behind her. Without preamble, Emerys marched down the corridor taking us to the queen's private quarters.

I could make out hushed voices from within when we reached the door. Emerys knocked sharply twice, and the voices quieted. A moment later, my mother opened the door to reveal a surprising face in the room with her.

Shunae.

The witch I'd faced during my first match of the tournament. The same woman who'd given me the information to get my phone working. I hadn't had any sense that she even knew the queen.

"I knew there was something different about you. Just didn't think it was a secret royal," she said upon seeing me.

"Yeah, surprised me, too." I took the time to study her properly, only to realize she sported the crown's colors of blue and silver. Her outfit was far more formal than anything I'd seen her in before. "You're part of the castle guard?"

"I told you about our delegation to the Seelie court," my mother interjected.

"You're the delegate?" I couldn't hide the disbelief in my tone.

"Oh, so you can be royalty, but I can't be a dignitary?" Shunae quipped.

"No, of course you can. Just wasn't what I pictured you doing is all. I figured you were more about solving things with your fists rather than your words," I admitted.

"Oh, don't worry. I'm good in a fight when the situation arises."

"Good to know."

"Morgan will be laying low while you're out of the kingdom," my mother explained.

It was a bald-faced lie, but a necessary one. The people who were representing the kingdom's interests needed to believe I was being kept out of sight until things blew over. If they had plausible deniability, it kept them just a little bit safer.

"If you've really been gone as long as Her Majesty says, you've got a lot to catch up on. There's a decent library on the second floor."

"Thanks."

"I'll coordinate with security and let you know when we're ready to head out," Shunae said, addressing my mother.

"Let's hope that these efforts will be fruitful," she replied.

Shunae moved past me and gave Emerys a small nod of acknowledgement before heading down the corridor we'd just come from. My mother ushered us inside, eying the packs with curiosity.

"It is probably safer the less I know about where you're going," she said before I could explain anything.

"You don't really think anyone is going to try and pry the information out of you," I scoffed. "You're the queen for fuck's sake. And like you've said, everyone is going to think I'm cooped up here."

"I appreciate your belief in me. But given the last three decades, I do not feel I can trust myself with the information."

The sadness in her eyes tugged at my heart. I stepped up and wrapped her in a tight embrace, ignoring the ache in my arm as I squeezed her tight. "I'm sorry you feel that way," I whispered.

She leaned back to study me. "I believe that

you'll accomplish whatever it is you are setting out to do."

"We don't know exactly where or what we'll be doing."

As I released my grip on her, I felt Excalibur bump against my hip. I'd forgotten I fastened it on before leaving with Emerys and Gethin earlier. "I know you don't want to know anything, but I can say that walking around with an actual sword is going to make us stand out."

"What about a transformation spell?" Gethin suggested. "Conceal it as something less conspicuous, so you don't have to leave it behind."

"The blade is dragon forged. Only a dragon of considerable power would be able to perform that level of magic," Emerys noted.

"Would someone with, say royal blood be strong enough?" I posed.

"Potentially," Emerys answered, drawing out the word as she gave me side eye. "Why do I get the sense you are about to suggest someone in particular?"

Gethin made a strangled sound. "Please don't tell me you think you can convince *him* to help."

"What am I missing?" my mother interjected.

"She thinks since she met Prince Taron once that she can just ask him for a favor," Gethin answered.

"I wasn't aware you'd met."

"During the tournament," I said, fixing Gethin with a look that clearly said, 'keep your mouth shut.' "But he seemed nice and his sister was pretty cool, too."

"Their family has been allies in the past. It is worth asking," Emerys agreed.

"I don't know if we have the time for official channels," my mother noted.

"Uh, I'm pretty sure I can go through some unofficial ones. Just give me until tomorrow. If he can't do it, then we'll figure something else out."

"Very well," my mother answered.

Now I just had to find a way back to Emerys' cabin before tomorrow morning and hope Taron stopped by for his morning swim.

EMERYS PROVIDED a portal for me bright and early the next morning with a reminder that I only had until evening to accomplish the task. I hardly slept the night before from the anticipation. It wasn't so much about whether Taron would be able to do what I asked. Rather what he thought of me knowing that I, too, was royalty now. Would he treat me any differently? Or would he refuse to speak to me for fear of igniting a diplomatic incident?

I arrived at the lakeside just as the sun crested over the tree line on the opposite shore. I turned my gaze skyward, hoping to see a large, winged silhouette, but only a few wispy clouds drifted into view. I began pacing, turning my attention to the unbroken surface of the water. I had no idea how long he could hold his breath or if dragons even needed to breathe underwater.

"Are you expecting something to emerge from the depths?" a familiar voice asked from beside me. "Or perhaps someone?"

I jumped, turning to find Taron, fully clothed, standing beside me. I hadn't heard him approach. I turned to try and gauge the direction he'd come. "Are all dragons bloody stealth ninjas?"

"Only those of us with practice," he replied. He tugged his shirt over his head, revealing his muscular torso and arms. "Taking me up on that offer of a swim together?"

Heat crept up the nape of my neck. I'd nearly forgotten about that particular offer the first day we'd met. It sounded like a lovely distraction, and I could already picture him naked, drawing me into the water. I could feel the ghost of his skin against my fingers. The vision sent a shiver through my core.

Get a grip Morgan.

I cleared my throat. "Maybe another time. I was actually hoping to ask for your help."

His face fell. "That's a shame. I'd have liked to go for a swim with Camelot's crown princess."

"So, you heard the news?"

"It was rather difficult not to," he answered. "When a ruling monarch makes an announcement that there's a new heir to the throne, it makes the news cycle everywhere."

"I'm still getting used to it all. Any tips?"

"Don't change who you are to fit what other people expect you to be."

"Believe me, I've been trying, but it's easier said than done. I feel like so many people are silently judging me. Like somehow, it's my fault Arthur was an imposter."

"You don't bear the responsibility for that. He was the one living a lie. Whether he knew it or not remains to be seen."

"Oh, I have no doubt he knew something.

Whether he knew he was actually the heir to another kingdom, well that I'm not sure."

"For what it's worth, I believe that King Uther is full of shit. I don't believe for a moment your mother would have taken a child, not if she'd known that happened to you."

"Thanks for that."

"You mentioned needing my help?" he prompted.

"If I tell you something, I need to know that you won't breathe a word of it to anyone. And don't ask me why I need it.

"Assuming it's not something illegal, I'll keep it in strictest confidence."

I tapped the hilt of the sword on my hip. "I need to know if there's a way to transform this into something more portable. I've heard dragons might know how to do something like that?"

"May I see it?"

My stomach did a flip at the request. Aside from my mother, no one else had handled Excalibur since I'd freed it from the stone. But if I wanted him to do anything, he'd need to lay hands on the blade. I unsheathed it and held it out.

He took it gently, laying the blade across his

right palm. "Remarkable. I'd heard stories of this sword from my childhood. It had been used by your ancestors in battle and it made their aim true. I can feel the power within it." He glanced up at me. "It feels like ... *you*."

"I haven't heard that one before," I mumbled.

"I just mean I could feel the power you let loose during your match with Arthur and this ... feels the same."

"Guess that makes sense. It's got my blood in it. Or something."

"So, that's how it's managed to stay out of the wrong hands for all these centuries," he muttered to himself.

"Do you think you can transform it? And have a way for me to turn it back if I need it?"

"With the right tools, yes. It is a delicate procedure, but I am willing to give it a go. For you." He cast a longing look at the water and passed the sword back to me. "But when this is over, we are going to have our swim."

"When what's over?" I played dumb.

He smiled. "Don't think I can't see you've got something brewing. I won't ask what it is, because I sense it's better I not know."

"You're a smart man," I answered. "I promise, when this is done, we're getting in that lake together."

"Good." He tossed his shirt to the ground. "Now, how do you feel about going for a ride?"

CHAPTER

SIX

Whatever I might have thought 'going for a ride' meant, I was so very wrong. Without ceremony, Taron stripped down naked, flashing me a flirty grin as he did so before taking a few steps back.

"You might want to back up a few steps," he said as he stretched his arms across his torso. "And would you mind grabbing those?"

He gestured to the pile of discarded clothes on the grass. I scooped them up and took several liberal paces away from him. The air around us grew charged with static electricity as his eyes glowed the same fiery orange I'd seen Talia's do during our match. His sister's transformation had been almost like a dance. Taron's was no less elegant. He hunched forward, tightening his abs and as he arched his shoulders back, his bare skin rippled with thick dark coppery scales. His legs lengthened and his feet shifted into clawed talons. His arms grew even more muscular as wings burst from his back.

His face was the last thing to change. Even seeing him with this distorted body didn't take away from the fact that he was a gorgeous man. His hair receded back into his skull, replaced by more scales. His nose elongated into a snout. The only things unchanged were his eyes. They regarded me with such intensity.

"Uh, if you're about to tell me to climb up, that's not happening," I called.

From the limited experience I'd had with Talia, I couldn't say for certain that he would be able to understand or respond to me in this form. He settled on his hind legs and held out his front talons. They were nearly as wide around as my torso. He waggled one talon as if to say, 'Come here.'

I hesitated, before securing Excalibur around my waist and pressing his bundle of clothes to my chest. He scooped me up into his front talons and nestled me close to his chest. I could make out the subtle difference in shading on the scales covering his belly from this distance.

With a puff of air through his nostrils, Taron launched us into the sky. I let out a yelp of surprise as the ground sped away from us faster than I'd ever traveled. I expected the air to turn my lashes to icicles the higher we got, but Taron stayed low enough that the air currents remained warm, if a bit damp.

It took a few minutes to feel comfortable enough to open my eyes and take in the landscape around us. I could just make out the castle in Camelot off in the distance to our left. But Taron wasn't headed that way. Instead, he turned on a dime, letting the currents buoy us in the opposite direction. The rolling hills and thick woodlands gave way to more open fields and rocky cliffs. I could feel my lips begin to chap from the wind and height as we glided over open bodies of water.

In the back of my mind, as I spotted lakes and rivers below us, I couldn't help but wonder what had drawn Taron to the lake near Emerys' cabin. I filed that curiosity away for a time when I wasn't worried about going off on some insane quest. Taron veered downward and I craned my neck to see where we were heading. From this high up it appeared to be an outcropping of rocks on an ocean shoreline.

The rockface came screaming up at us, so fast my entire body tensed and my jaw clamped shut in an effort to brace for impact. Instead, Taron's wings slowed to a lazy flap and his body arced, pushing his hind talons ahead of us. They dug into the rough surface beneath, slowing our forward momentum, but not enough to send me jolting out of his arms. He carefully lowered me to the ground, and I tumbled free of his embrace. I managed not to land too awkwardly and avoided my injured shoulder, while still clutching his clothing. Realizing he'd likely need them; I laid them between us and shuffled back as much as I could.

His transition back to human state was less alluring. This time I was conscious of the sound of bones cracking and joints snapping back into a proper human shape. Still, his eyes never left mine as he made the transition back. In fact, he didn't break our locked gazes while he dressed either.

"So, that happened," I said dumbly.

"You did remarkably well for your first time," he said and offered me a hand.

"Mind telling me where we are exactly?"

"The edge of the territory between your kingdom and mine," he replied.

"Do people know you like to slip across the border to take a dip in the morning?"

"The fact it is in another domain is precisely why I do it. Granted, if for some reason we had not been on good terms with your mother, I'd have found somewhere else to indulge."

"Hooray for political allies," I muttered.

He guided me down the uneven footholds in the rockface to a patch of dirt in an otherwise sandy shoreline. Something told me he'd used this landing spot on more than one occasion.

"This way," he said, pulling me around the edge of the outcropping to reveal the mouth of a cave.

What's with people and caves?

"You'll need to crouch a bit, but it's only for about a quarter of a meter," he explained.

I ducked my head and followed him into the cave. It was more of a cavern as we got farther inside. The passage widened considerably and when we emerged my jaw dropped. From the exterior I would have assumed this was just another shallow cave like the Crystal Cave. Maybe there was magic in place to make it bigger on the inside or the cavern really was this spacious. Somehow lights hung from various spots in the ceiling. I could trace the electrical wiring to a box on one of the far walls. There were various metal working benches laid out in neat rows within the vast space.

"Holy shit," I breathed.

"Welcome to my workshop," Taron said. I could hear the excitement in his tone.

"How'd you get all of this in here?"

"You are aware magic exists, yes?"

"Stupid question, got it."

I did a slow spin, taking in the rest of the space. I spotted numerous finished sculptures sitting on a table nearby and gravitated toward them. They appeared to be made of every metal imaginable from silver and pewter to gold and steel.

Gorgeous. Lives in a cave. Hoards treasure.

"You really are a dragon," I said with a snort.

"What is that supposed to mean?"

"Don't tell me people here haven't heard stories about dragons living in caves, protecting their precious troves." I waved my hands around to signify the surroundings. "You're living the stereotype."

"I do not live in a cave," he scoffed.

I spotted a single bed shoved in a corner. Based on the disturbed sheets and the rumpled pillow, I begged to differ. I jabbed a finger at it. "Want to say that again?"

"I never said I didn't sleep here on occasion. It's easier if I'm working late. But I do not live here."

"Okay, I take it back," I said with a laugh. "So, what tools do you need to turn this into something less conspicuous?" I patted Excalibur's scabbard.

"Well, I needed a forge," he replied and ushered me to a large contraption near the back of the cave. I glanced up to see a hole had been carved into the roof.

"Aren't forges used to melt things?" I asked, my voice cracking with unease.

"Technically, yes."

My left hand tightened on the hilt of the sword as I said, "I'm not sure I like that idea."

"You want me to transform it. It needs to be malleable for me to do that. I swear it isn't going to damage the sword."

I wanted to trust his word. But I was also terrified I'd mess this up and have to go slinking back to Camelot to tell the people who were counting on me that I'd let Excalibur be melted down.

"Morgan, on my honor, I will not do anything to harm this blade," Taron said, his tone taking on a serious edge.

My hand shook as I pulled the blade free. On reflex, my fingers tightened around the sapphire-encrusted pommel. Maybe the sword could sense my apprehension.

"Lay it just there," Taron instructed.

It took all of my willpower to part with the sword. Taron ushered me to stay back and bent beneath the forge. He sucked in a breath before breathing out fire. It burned white hot, but I could see sparks of something purple and green within it. He straightened and as he did so the skin on his hands turned rough and scaly.

Excalibur glittered in the heat, and I could feel a thick sheen of sweat break out over my entire body. Taron didn't appear affected by the sudden change in temperature.

"Now, I am going to need your verbal consent to begin the process," he said.

"I consent to you not destroying my sword."

He fixed me with a disapproving glare. "Without the snark, if you would be so kind?"

"Fine ... I consent."

He reached down and picked up a small knife and held it out to me. "It's also going to need a bit of your blood and magic."

"Why does everything need my damn blood?" I groaned.

"Because it is the easiest price to pay," he

replied.

I let him prick my right index finger and squeezed a few drops of blood onto the blade's surface. The metallic surface shimmered as it recognized my connection to it again.

"You might want to shield your eyes for this part," he warned.

I raised a hand to partially obscure my view. I wasn't going to completely look away. I needed to know what he was doing. The sword turned molten, burning a vivid orange. That's when Taron scooped it up in his scale-covered hands. I felt a rush of energy as he twisted the malleable metal and gems.

My heart leapt into my throat, making it almost impossible to swallow as he took a hammer to the sword. Every strike against the anvil sent a jolt of fear through my body.

Just as I was beginning to regret the choice to ask Taron for this particular favor, he settled the reconfigured object into a barrel to cool. I didn't exhale until he'd pulled it out to reveal he'd molded it into a bracelet.

He studied me for a moment before tapping my left wrist. "Here."

He slid the bracelet on. I turned it over, finding a smaller version of the sapphire that sat at Excalibur's hilt. I closed my eyes, reaching within myself to let my magic come to the surface. Limes tickled my tastebuds and the bracelet warmed to the touch.

"To reconstitute it into its true form, you need only hold the gem and exert a fraction of power," Taron instructed. "It will only respond to your magic."

Please let this work.

Letting my magic out was the easy part. Something about being around Excalibur made my power easier to channel. I pressed my index finger to the small gem on the bracelet and let out a surprised gasp as the metal unwound from around my wrist. It kept elongating and extending into the hilt, and then the blade of the sword. The sapphire grew in size too, until it fit into the hilt properly.

I studied the blade for any signs it was damaged or altered. Everything appeared in order. I gave it a quick wave around, forcing Taron to shuffle back out of range. "Sorry."

"To return it to its concealed form, you simply do the same thing," he said, recovering his composure in an instant. "Now, it should serve you in whatever capacity you require."

"Thank you. I'm really grateful for your help."

To test the magic—and because I really didn't

want a giant length of steel separating us, I pressed the sapphire with my left thumb. It shrank back down into the band encircling my wrist with a soft 'click.' Taron closed the distance between us, and I could feel myself getting lost in his gaze.

"Wherever you are going, please do not go alone."

"You don't have to worry about that. I'm royalty now. I travel with an entourage." He didn't need to know it was only Gethin and Emerys who'd be joining me.

"Yes, I suppose that is true. Although it would seem you are skilled at evading them when you want to as well."

"I got permission to wander freely. Just this once."

"Pity. We'll have to practice your ... how did you put it ... stealth ninja skills upon your return."

I beamed at him, silently willing him to lean in and kiss me. It was a wholly inappropriate desire given the circumstances. Yet, after what I'd gone through in the last few weeks, I could do with a bit of male attention.

"I should probably get back. We're meant to be leaving soon and I did promise I'd be back before dark."

"Of course."

He led the way out of the cavern and back into the daylight. I stumbled on the rocks as my eyes tried to adjust to the sudden brightness of the sky above us. The sun had moved significantly and was nearly overhead. Time had lost all meaning within the walls of Taron's workshop. In front of me, Taron turned back to offer a hand and I held tight as he hoisted me up.

"Can I ask you something?" I blurted as he began to shed clothing.

"Why not?"

"What's it feel like to turn into a dragon?"

"You know, no one's ever asked me that before."

"Oh, come on. I'm sure plenty of people have wondered."

"Most of the people in our kingdom are shifters, too. It isn't something that's openly discussed."

"Oh ... I didn't mean to bring up something that's so personal. Forget I asked."

"No, it's just not something I'd ever really taken the time to consider. It's just commonplace. Everyone does it, so we don't really talk about it." He paused in the removal of his pants. "Emotionally speaking, it's like taking off a mask I wear every day, revealing the truth and power within. Physically, it's a bit like going through a growth period all at once. Uncomfortable the first few times you do it, but the discomfort doesn't last."

"Thank you for sharing," I said.

"And thank you for asking. I can tell you are going to be quite the inquisitive ruler one day."

"I don't know about that. One day feels like so far off. I'm just looking to make it through tomorrow to be honest."

"Well, let's get you back to Camelot, so you can begin that journey into tomorrow."

SEVEN

That night, I dreamt of the mysterious cup the cave had shown me. Without more context, it felt like such a random piece of information to pass along. I woke before the sun and stayed in bed, staring at the ceiling, trying to puzzle out what lies ahead of me. It appeared the compass was pointing back through the barrier to the world I'd been raised in, but that was an enormous expanse to search for a single item. It didn't help I was the only one to have seen the vision. It wasn't like I could just share my it with Emerys and Gethin so we had three pairs of eyes keeping a look out.

By the time my phone's clock read seven, I was out of bed and dressed. At this point it had become a glorified timepiece. But deep down I still help out hope Jules would find way to get in touch. My arm gave a few small protestations at being used for the first time in a week, but I pushed through the discomfort. Standing in front of the mirror, I slid the compass over my head, letting it rest against my chest. Realizing it might give us away, or at the very least draw unwanted attention, I tucked it beneath my shirt, shivering as the cool metal touched my skin. I settled the fabric of my top and caught sight of the bracelet now adorning my wrist.

I couldn't help but press my finger to the tiny gem, taking a step back as I did so to give Excalibur room to expand. Part of me still didn't believe the magic would work now that I wasn't in Taron's workshop. Thankfully, the metal elongated as both it and the gem reconstituted itself into the sword.

The sword seemed to vibrate in my hand, and I pressed the flat of the blade to my forehead. An odd sense of connection washed over me, accompanied by what I could only describe as relief. Maybe the sword was just as nervous as me.

"This feels so bizarre," I announced to the empty air as I pressed the gem in the hilt and it retracted, shrinking into the bracelet again.

Wasting no more time, I made my way down to the kitchen. To my surprise, I made the trek without getting lost. I found Gethin already occupying the space, packing a bag with food.

"Mate, you do know they've got food where we're headed," I reminded him.

Gethin looked at me, his glasses slipping down his nose. "I just want to be prepared. We have no idea where we're meant to go once we cross through the barrier." He set down a tart, the glaze on the top still glistening. "When I'm nervous, I focus on food."

I'd hoped his nerves would have subsided after our last conversation. "Just make sure you've still got room for the rest of your stuff."

I reached over and picked up a peach from the counter. He gave me an eyeroll, but didn't stop me as I bit into it. The soft flesh came away easy and juice dribbled undignified down my chin.

"I thought I might find you both down here," Emerys said, appearing in the doorway to my left.

I wiped the juice with the back of my hand before Gethin could pass me a napkin. She gave me a disapproving look. I offered a shrug in return and took another bite of the fruit. I savored the sharpness to the taste. It was far better than the ones I had in London. My brain went down a mental rabbit hole of wondering whether this realm's natural magic had something to do with it.

"We should eat quickly and depart," Emerys said.

"Shunae and the delegation aren't even leaving until this afternoon," Gethin protested.

I pivoted to look at him. "And how exactly do you know that? I didn't even know that."

"I may have ... uh, eavesdropped a little."

"Just hope she didn't see you. Remember she tailed you looking for tech magic."

His cheeks flushed at the mention of his less than stealthy attempt to find someone to make my phone work. "I get wanting to hit the road and all, but wouldn't it be better if we stayed until they were gone. That way they could say the last time they saw us we were here?" I proposed.

"I've already conferred with the Queen. She agrees we should leave this morning."

Part of me was offended I hadn't been included in that discussion. After all, I was the one about to go off on some quest. Sure, Emerys was coming, too. But it wasn't her destiny we were following. Still, another part was relieved that the two were on speaking terms again.

"Fine. We'll head out once we've all had a chance to eat and get some decent coffee."

"Is there anything else you can tell us about

what you saw?" Gethin asked as he fired up the burners on the stove.

"There's really not much more to tell. I saw myself leading a bunch of women in some fight. I assume against Arthur. And then I saw a vision of some cup."

"Can you describe it?" Emerys pressed.

"It was sort of gold or amber I think." I closed my eyes, trying to picture it. "There was something in the middle of it ... Like a stone."

"Maybe a memory spell would help," Gethin offered amongst the clanging of pans.

I opened my eyes and looked at him. "A what spell?"

"Memory spell."

"It took you a good five years to even begin to master that magic," Emerys reminded him.

"Yeah, but I'm not the future ruler of Camelot, descended from a noble bloodline full of insanely powerful magic."

"What would I have to do? And how exactly would it help?"

"A memory spell would allow you to project your memory beyond yourself. We would be able to see what you see," Emerys explained.

"Any memory?"

"Theoretically."

I swallowed the lump in my throat. "And let's say I could in fact do this, how is it going to help? You can't exactly copy it into *your* memory." *Wait. Can she?*

She gave me a wry smile. "I am nearly a millennium in age, Morgan. I can do a great many things you could not even begin to dream of."

"Right, well in that case, let's give it a try." I held up a finger to stop her next words. "After coffee."

I settled onto a stool at the center island and watched as Gethin put together three delicious-smelling omelettes. Somehow, he knew exactly what to put in each. I looked around the space, only then realizing that the kitchen staff weren't present. Surely, they had to be preparing for the day?

"Did the queen give us free reign in here or something?"

"Yes," Emerys answered simply. She joined us at the island and made a grabbing gesture at my wrist. "May I see?"

I held up my wrist so she could inspect the bracelet. She prodded the metal, ran her fingertip along the sapphire acting as the clasp. "Beautiful craftsmanship."

"It was pretty intense to witness. I had a minor heart attack when I watched him melt it down."

"One day you will have to tell me the true origin of your acquaintance with the dragon prince."

"It's kind of a long story," I said.

"She interrupted his skinny dipping," Gethin blabbed.

"Okay, I guess it's not that long …"

I expected Emerys to give me another disapproving look. Instead, the smile she offered was one of amusement. "I don't know how long he thought he was going to get away with that unseen."

"He's been seen all right," I said with a grin of my own. "And I'm not going to lie, I didn't hate it."

"Dragons are complicated creatures. Believe me when I say that I speak from experience," Emerys said with a sly grin.

Noted.

"Breakfast is served," Gethin announced louder than necessary, setting the plates down on the island's surface with a clatter.

For a brief time, all conversation ceased as we ate. Gethin had brought over a carafe of coffee with cream and sugar. I poured myself a cup and downed half of it before I'd even eaten a bite of food. The caffeine hit my system as I was finishing the omelette. Finally, I felt like a functioning human being again.

I stood, taking my dirty dishes to the sink and began to rinse them out of habit. Not that the staff would likely care if I hadn't cleaned up after myself. I slid the plate and utensils into an industrial washer and returned to my half empty cup of coffee. I nursed the remainder while Gethin and Emerys finished their meals.

"So, are you immortal?" I asked.

"No. I am just as mortal as you. I have simply been gifted with an elongated span on this earth. And in my long life, I have been fortunate in not having suffered any grave illness. I believe it was the universe's way of ensuring that I was here to guide you on your path."

"And to train Gethin, too," I said.

"Yes. And to guide his path, too." She set aside her plate. "Now, are you ready to begin the memory spell?"

"Ready as I'll ever be I suppose."

"Should we be doing this in the kitchen? The Queen might have given us some time in here, but that won't last forever," Gethin suggested.

"We should retire to my quarters," Emerys said.

She led the way to a floor I hadn't explored in a

tower that boasted a large circular room. She pointed to the bed. "Sit."

I sat, absently playing with the band around my wrist. I stopped short when my thumb was about to brush against the sapphire. I didn't think this was a situation that called for Excalibur. At least I hoped not. I stopped fidgeting, clamping both hands down on my knees.

"Before you even attempt to conjure the memory around us, you need to find it within yourself. Allow it to fill you up, put yourself back in that moment," Emerys instructed.

I closed my eyes, allowing my mind to take me back to the cave and the time before the gift of the compass. I watched myself study the images shifting on the water's surface.

"I'm there," I said, my voice sounding far away even to my ears.

"Allow yourself to summon your power and project the image outward beyond yourself," Emerys instructed.

Let them see.

I pushed, willing the world around me to take on what I saw in my mind's eye. When I opened my eyes, another version of me sat on a rocky cave floor in front of me. The cave walls and ceiling flickered against the castle's stone like a film projector, but it was enough for Emerys and Gethin to see.

"Let it play out," Emerys said.

"Uh, play?" I muttered.

The images began moving as if we were watching a projected film on a screen. I watched myself react to the image of the women falling into ranks behind me. Then the image of the cup appeared.

"Can you stop it?" Gethin asked.

"Stop?"

The image flickered, but didn't change. The scent of my magic coated the inside of my nostrils, and everything was sour when I swallowed. A dull ache began at the base of my skull. Out of the corner of my eye, I watched as Gethin produced a sketchpad and began drawing.

A man of many talents.

Emerys reached out and touched the memory of the cup. It appeared to glitch and then for a split second I was seeing double. That vanished back into one and a few seconds later Emerys stepped back.

"I think I've got it," Gethin announced.

"You may let the spell fade," Emerys added.

All of the tension that had been building in my body loosened as I let the power ebb away. The ache in my skull remained though. The price of doing a new spell taking its toll. The jolt of energy I'd gotten from the coffee appeared to vanish with the cave. *Damn it.*

I took a few minutes to gather myself before we made our way down to the first floor. I stopped outside the dining room, picking up on my mother's voice from within. It didn't feel right to leave without letting her know. I think that's what daughters did when they went off for a while, they told their mums.

"Just give me a minute," I told my travel companions.

I walked in to find her in conversation with a woman I didn't know. She wasn't wearing the uniform of the castle staff. But she didn't look like she belonged to the Seelie court and I couldn't tell whether she was a dragon either.

"Morning," my mother greeted, as if this was an ordinary encounter between us.

"Morning." I stared at the other woman, unsure if it was safe to speak openly in front of her.

"This is Jamilla Corant," my mother said, as if the name should have some meaning to me. "She is a member of the council."

"It is an honor to meet you, Princess," she said, offering a bow.

"Morgan is fine," I said through a thin-lipped smile. "I'm sorry to interrupt, but I was hoping to have a word with my mum … just us two."

"Of course. I am sure you two have a lot to catch up on, "Jamilla said with a smile.

I waited until the door had closed behind her to speak again. "Something I should know?"

"Nothing to worry about. She's an ally. I am sure there will be time for you to get to know everyone on the council. You will need their support one day, after all."

"Right. Well, I wanted to let you know we're going."

"Yes. Emerys advised me you'd be leaving today."

"I meant like now."

"Oh." After a beat, she added, "I thought we agreed it was best that I do not know the details."

"We did. But it felt strange to just leave without at least telling you. You know kinda like the sort of things mums and daughters do."

Her face fell. "Of course, it is." She stood and rounded the table, folding me into a tentative hug. "Have a good trip."

"I promise I won't be gone for thirty years this time," I replied.

"See that you aren't."

She released me from the embrace, and I returned to the corridor to find Emerys and Gethin waiting. We made our way to the bowels of the castle and out the same way we'd gone two days earlier. Emerys sketched a circle in the air and the woods by the Crystal Cave appeared within its confines. I led the way this time, moving confidently through the brush and foliage to stand by the mouth of the cave. I waited for my companions to join me before I pulled the compass out to confirm the direction we needed to go.

The needle spun before settling straight ahead. For good measure, the metal pulled away from my body as if drawn by a magnet. Back through the barrier we went.

EIGHT

I expected the change in the world to be more pronounced as we made reentry to the realm, I'd called home for thirty years. Aside from the air taking on a hint of fossil fuels, the only real sign we'd left Camelot behind was the shift from woodlands to open fields. I looked around, my bearings off kilter for a moment.

"Wait, we're in ... Ireland?"

"As far as I am aware, there is only one such gate connecting this realm to Camelot's," Emerys answered.

"It looks so peaceful," Gethin noted.

"As I told Morgan on our travels here, this place is the home of great power. Battles have been waged on these hills."

"It's apparently a tourist destination now," I added, noticing the visitor fence and barricades in the distance. "Come on, I'm pretty sure they don't let the visitors out this far. We're going to need to blend in."

I took off at a brisk walk, expecting them to keep up with me. I didn't have a bloody clue where we were meant to go now that we'd arrived, but I had to believe it wasn't just to hang around here all day. A gaggle of folks with their phones held aloft came into view around a roped off area.

"This way," I hissed, pulling my phone free from my pocket. I shifted the weight of my pack onto both shoulders and held up my phone, pretending to take a few photos with the crowd. Thankfully, Emerys' peasant top and long flowing skirt fit in with the crowd. Gethin's trousers and linen shirt looked a little more out of place, but their clothes didn't scream 'outsider.'

No one appeared to pay us any mind. That was good. Even though we were careful on our exit from the castle, there was still a possibility someone could have seen us leave. In theory, my magic should be able to detect any hidden tails. But that assumed my magic was working properly across the boundary.

History suggested I'd be as crippled and cut off as I'd been my entire life. Still, I let out a bit of power and the intent to reveal any unwanted companions. To my relief, my magic jumped to attention the moment I needed it. I glanced over my right shoulder, but nothing stood out. A check over the left held a similar absence of anything nefarious.

Good.

As I let the magic die down, my wrist warmed and I caught Excalibur glowing a faint pale blue. Maybe the sword had been part of what I'd been missing all along. Whatever the reason, I was glad to have full command of my magic now.

"We need to determine where we're meant to be searching for this cup," Emerys said in my ear.

"It looks more like a chalice," Gethin offered. I gave him a sideways glance. "What? It's ornate, clearly well crafted. Cup just feels so ... mundane a term."

"Whatever we call it, Emerys is right. We need to figure out where we go from here," I said.

Two pairs of eyes fell on me.

"Right, I'm the one leading the quest. I should probably be the one to sort out where we're headed."

Consulting the compass seemed a solid first

step, if an incomplete one. It could give us a direction, but that didn't really narrow it down. Still, it was worth a shot. I tugged the compass free from beneath my shirt and opened it, holding it flat in my palm. The needle, which had been pointing west before, now indicated more southwest.

Only moderately useful.

I reached up to close the compass and the moment my other hand touched the metal, my head filled with a flurry of images. *A clock tower. A smear of colors—maybe purple or blue—on a sign. A bell above a shop door. A shelf of books.*

The only thing that looked remotely familiar was the clock tower. But I couldn't be entirely certain I knew where it was. But I knew someone who might.

"What just happened?" Gethin's voice drew me back to our surroundings.

"I think the compass was giving me some clues of where we need to head." He looked at me expectantly. "It was all a blur, and they didn't really make sense. None of it seemed particularly clear. But we're not far from London, and my mate Jules is brilliant at puzzles. If anyone can help us riddle this out, it's her."

Besides, I couldn't not see her now that we were

back in the area. I had to assuage my guilt about leaving her behind the first time.

Our quest was about to become a party of four.

"Come on, your powers got you to London last time. Put those ancient skills to good use," I complained as we waited for the ferry that would take us across to Liverpool.

"I have used the portal's magic far too much in recent days. It requires time to recharge," Emerys said.

I wanted to call her on her bullshit. It hadn't looked like it needed a charge any of the times she'd used it. "You were the one who insisted we leave so damn early. We're wasting time waiting for the bloody ferry. And what, a train next?"

It felt counterproductive to waste a whole day on travel. Not to mention the fact I was rapidly running out of money and didn't want to charge the expenses. Not when I had no idea when or if I'd ever be back to pay the bill.

"I cannot create a portal. End of discussion," Emerys answered sharply. "I am going to check our departure time."

I leaned over to Gethin and said, "It can't be that hard. You've seen her do it loads of times, right?"

"Please don't," he sighed. "I've honestly never seen her use it this much. And I couldn't even begin to tell you the mechanics of the magic. How it works to get you where you need to be, especially when you've never been there before."

"Weren't you saying earlier that I am from a supremely powerful bloodline destined to rule?"

"Yes, but … "

"Then why can't I do it?"

"Because you're not her."

No, I wasn't.

"Alright, fine," I said in a huff,

I pulled my phone from my pocket only to realize it was dead. Apparently, the change in realms hadn't done it any favors yet again. I couldn't even let Jules know we were coming. Emerys returned and pointed out that our ride had finally arrived.

The salt air did nothing to improve my mood as we crossed back to England's shore. The sun began its descent by the time we reached the dock in Liverpool.

"Look, I'm running out of money. I don't know if I've got enough to get us three train tickets back to London. If you don't want to do the portal thing, then let me try," I proposed once we were clear of any potential eavesdroppers.

Emerys opened her mouth and the determined look in her eyes told me she was about to argue. After a moment, her expression turned to one of resignation. "It is ancient magic, far older than either of us. I cannot hope to teach you to control it in a matter of years, let alone minutes or hours. However, if you insist on attempting it, I will give you instructions. If only to prove that you are not yet ready to learn this."

"Great. Let's give it a go then."

I led our trio away from the train depot to a more secluded area that appeared to be used for loading cargo train cars. It would do. I shook my hands out, momentarily wondering if actually holding Excalibur would be a good move. Then I realized we were still in a public place and waving around a sword was not a smart move.

"Before you begin you must first envision your destination. Picture it clearly in your mind," Emerys said.

Okay, that seemed simple enough. I wanted to get to Julayne, so I pictured the hall in front of her flat. At this time of day most of her neighbors would be at work, leaving us the ability to pop in unseen. I knew for a fact none of the building's interior had cameras. The landlord was too cheap for that sort of security measure.

"Got it," I said softly.

"Now, you must create the portal. It must be a perfect circle," Emerys continued.

That felt oddly specific. And probably just an attempt to see if it would trip me up. I hadn't been paying much attention to whether her portals were perfectly round and symmetrical. I was no artist, but even I could manage a circle.

I started at the twelve position on a clock face and traced my way past the three, six, and nine before coming back to the top again. She hadn't specifically said to pour power into it, but that part seemed obvious. When I opened my eyes, I found a weak shimmer of a circle in front of me. Nothing like the vibrant doorways she'd created. I could sort of make out the carpeting in the corridor outside of Julayne's flat. But it could also have been the sunlight reflecting off our surroundings.

"I can do this," I insisted.

I held my left hand out, palm up and fingers splayed. I grasped my right hand around the wrist, making sure each finger had a point of contact on the bracelet. I might not need to magically unsheathe the blade, but I was beginning to see that it could offer me a power boost when needed.

The shimmer became a full-on glow and the space within resolved firmly into the corridor outside her flat. I barely contained the shriek of excitement that I'd actually managed it. I silently noted the look of amazement and shock that colored Emerys' cheeks.

"Right, I'll pop through first and you two follow," I said.

"You're the one fueling the spell. It's entirely possible if you go through first, it closes behind you," Gethin said, his voice inching towards falsetto.

"Gethin is correct. It would be safer if we go first."

"Fine. But don't go knocking on her door without me. She doesn't know you and given the fact she was attacked outside her building by magic wielding, pointy eared assassins, she's likely to be a bit jumpy."

"Got it," Gethin croaked before shuffling forward and sidestepping through the portal.

Emery looked as if she was about to say something, but thought better of it. As she moved through the portal, the strain began to take a toll on me. My body ached, my vision blurred, and blood rushed in my ears.

Time was running out for me to keep the portal open and make it through safely. Casting one last look around, I thrust myself forward and stumbled through the portal. It snapped shut behind me as I staggered unceremoniously into Gethin. He steadied me, but I reached out to put a hand on the wall. Nausea ripped through me, and it was all I could do to not make a mess of the corridor.

When the feeling had passed, I flipped the corner of the mat in front of the door to find the spare key. A sense of unease washed over me as I slid it into the lock and opened the door.

"Jules, it's Morgan. You in?" I called.

The flat was empty. In fact, it appeared that Jules hadn't been home in a couple of days. That was strange. She hated crashing anywhere, but in her own bed. But the phone charger she left on the front table was missing, as were her car keys. A quick inspection of her bedroom revealed she'd packed a suitcase in a hurry too.

Well, shit.

"Maybe she had a trip planned you didn't know about?" Gethin suggested.

"No. This feels like she left in a hurry. Something's wrong." Instinctively, I reached for my phone only to remember a moment later the battery was dead. "Look, my flat's just up the way. I can get a charge on this, grab a few other things, and then I can reach out to her then."

"I'm sure she's okay," Gethin said as we made our way down the back stairs.

I said nothing as we traced the same path I'd taken that horrible night two weeks ago that led me to my ruined apartment, and Aunt Nim's dying words. Part of me wanted to turn the other way and not go there. I was terrified of what I'd find. Still, my feet carried me back home.

I stopped outside the building, staring up at the façade. I was overcome with memories of celebrating holidays and birthdays here with Aunt Nim and Jules by my side. The two people who'd loved me unconditionally. One was gone forever and the other might be in danger now. Both because of me.

"Something wrong?" Gethin whispered.

"No. Just, I honestly didn't think I'd be coming back here after everything that happened."

He reached down and took my hand in his, giving it a firm squeeze. "You're not alone."

"I needed that."

I gave Gethin's hand a return squeeze and broke

contact, pulling the door to the building open with my other hand. We progressed up to my flat and I stopped just outside. I couldn't explain how I knew it, but the flat wasn't empty.

It should have been. Or at the very least, it shouldn't have had anything living inside. And yet I got the distinct impression there was something alive beyond the door. Had the police come and found Aunt Nim's body? Could they be lying in wait, ready to accuse me of murder? Or had the assassins who'd actually murdered her come back to finish the job, hoping one day I'd return?

There was only one way to find out.

I turned the handle and the door swung inward. I made it into the entryway of the flat, leading to the kitchen when a violent roar erupted from what had been Aunt Nim's bedroom. I turned in the nick of time to find Julayne wielding a cricket bat, ready to slam it into my head.

"Jules!" I shouted, holding up my hands to catch the bat on its descent.

She stopped mid-motion, staring at me in utter shock. It took her a minute to fully register that I was standing in front of her. But once she did, she cast the bat aside and flung herself at me, wrapping her limbs around me like a small child clinging to its mother.

"What are you doing here?" Jules demanded once she'd relinquished her vice-like grip on me.

"I could ask you the same thing." I nodded toward the discarded bat. "What's with the bat? You hate cricket."

"Lonnie two doors down from me heard I'd phoned the police and insisted I take it for protection." She let out a breath. "And to be honest, after that fire throwing bloke, I didn't quite trust my magic."

"Well, that explains the bat, but what are you doing here? Your flat looks like you left in a hurry."

"I figured those arseholes might come back looking for you. I wanted to be here if they did. Give you a fighting chance."

It was my turn to pull her into a hug. "God, I missed you, Jules. I've got so much to tell you."

"How about you start with who your friends are?"

I cleared my throat. "Right. Jules, this is Gethin. And that is Emerys. Oh, and I am now legally the recognized heir to the throne of Camelot."

"Fuck, you go away for two weeks and get all fancy on me. Not that I ever doubted it."

I knew she hadn't. She'd been the true believer in Aunt Nim's stories even after all these years. I had so many questions to ask her and so much to fill her in on. But we'd come here for a purpose.

"We're here, because we're looking for something." I gestured for Gethin's sketchpad. He handed it over and I showed her the image he'd drawn. "It's a cup."

"Chalice," he corrected.

"Right, chalice. Hell, call it the Holy Grail if you want. Whatever it is, I'm meant to find it."

"Holy Grail might not be too far off," Jules said. "And I think I know where to start looking."

CHAPTER

NINE

Getting out of the flat took longer than I'd meant it to. Being back here again—once I'd gotten over the initial shock of Julayne's cricket bat welcome—brought up more emotion than I was prepared to work through in the span of a few minutes. I sat on my bed, trying hard not to absolutely lose my shit. I could hear Emerys and Gethin talking in low tones in the kitchen. Julayne stood in the doorway to my bedroom eyeing me.

"I really never thought I'd be coming back here," I said softly. "It looks like nothing happened."

Julayne pushed off from the doorframe and came to sit at my side. "I knew how it would look if the police came snooping and found remnants of a struggle. So, I cleaned up as best I could."

"What happened to Aunt Nim's body?"

"Body? She was gone when I got here."

That unnerved me, but it made a macabre sort of sense. The assassins had talked about taking both of our bodies with them as proof of a job well done. They must have managed to take her body back. Whether that had been before or after Emerys and I had made it to Camelot's soil, I couldn't say.

"Sometimes I wake up and think this must have all been a dream. That Aunt Nim will be standing in the kitchen arguing with the coffee maker like always," I whispered.

Julayne pulled me into a tight embrace. "I can't imagine losing her like you did. But her stories were real. You are a princess. One with a mission. So, buck up Morgan Le Fey, because you're going to need to use some of that royal charisma where we're going."

I stuffed a few extra clothes and my phone charger in my pack along with a small silver-framed photo of Aunt Nim and I before leaving the flat behind. We didn't speak until we reached the street. I cast my eyes about, trying to guess where we'd be headed and how. Julayne caught my attention when she clicked the unlock button on her car's key fob and the headlights flashed five cars down on the right-hand side of the road.

"Please tell me we aren't going to take multiple modes of transit to get where we're going," I said as I approached the vehicle.

Julayne threw me a sideways glance. "Not last I checked. But something tells me there's a story behind that."

"I'll fill you in on the way," I answered and pressed the button to pull the front passenger seat forward to allow Gethin and Emerys to squeeze into the back seat.

"So, you're telling me there is a magical doorway between this world and another one in the middle of nowhere Ireland ... and it's been there for decades. Nim never bothered to mention it or even take you?" Julayne recapped as she pulled into the flow of evening traffic out of the city.

"The gate has been there far longer than decades," Emerys interjected from her spot crammed behind the driver's seat. "I cannot say for certain when the phenomenon first began, but it has existed for at least the better part of eight centuries."

Julayne let out a snort. "Eight hundred years. And you just happen to know this because ... what, you were there?"

I caught the stern look on Emerys' face in the rearview mirror. "Yes. I was."

"Uh, she's not joking," I added to stave off Julayne's protest about Emerys being full of shit.

"Remind me to ask you about your beauty regimen. I want to look that good when I'm old."

"Living for centuries has its downsides," Emerys murmured before turning her attention to the world passing us by through the window.

"As to why my Aunt Nim never brought me, I don't know. I would guess she didn't think it was safe to bring me back as a child. Or maybe her magic wasn't strong enough to get us back."

The moment Julayne shifted the car from the smooth paved city streets to the less maintained dirt and gravel of the country I realized our destination. I let out a groan.

"Jules, you can't be serious. You can't really think they'd help us."

"Why not?" she countered. "You want to find something old as dirt, talk to the people who are old as dirt." She turned to look at Emerys for a split second. "No offense."

"Who are you talking about?" Gethin piped up, leaning as far forward as the seat belt would allow.

"The Practitioner's Council," Julayne and I answered in unison.

"They're a bunch of crusty old magic blowhards who've been around for ages. They like to tell everyone what to do and how to use their magic," I explained.

"They also have an impressive amount of magical history and texts on the occult that you can't find in your everyday library," Julayne added. "If there's going to be anything useful about the Grail, it's going to be there."

"But they're going to want to get involved," I pointed out.

"You let me handle the stuffy snobs," Jules said with a grin. "Like I said, Princess, you've got to use that royal gumption to your advantage now."

"I've got about as much charisma as an old sock," I grumbled.

While I was growing up, Aunt Nim had been openly distrustful of the Council. I'd asked her why when I was old enough to understand the concept of a governing body. She'd insisted she disliked the centralization of knowledge. She felt they guarded magic's secrets too strictly. To her, magic should be practiced openly and without fear. The Council had been more restrictive in my youth.

Now, I wondered whether she had feared them finding out she wasn't from this world. It would have raised more questions. Did the Council know about Camelot and the realm beyond the Crystalline Gate? If they found out Aunt Nim's true nature, would they have allowed her to raise me or would the only parental figure I'd ever known have been snatched away from me, leaving me abandoned and orphaned? Unsurprisingly, I'd adopted her dislike of the Council. Besides, growing up, no one but Jules had ever believed I was meant to rule some far-off kingdom.

"You may not be a leader, yet, but you were born for it," Gethin offered from behind me.

"I know you're trying to be encouraging, but it really isn't helping," I replied and rested my head against the window.

The dirt and gravel crunched beneath the tires as Julayne maneuvered the car along the path leading to the large manor house that served as the Council's headquarters. Another reason I wasn't fond of them—they insisted on keeping their primary residence in the middle of fucking nowhere. The people they governed might have magic, but portals weren't a thing here. So, if anyone needed them, you either had to pay for petrol or a ride share to get all the way out here. That tended to result in the poorer practitioners being kept at the fringes of the magical community.

Behind me, I heard Gethin let out a gasp as we pulled to a stop in the large circular drive. The house had been used for evacuating women and children during the World War II London Blitz. I knew for a fact that some TARDIS, fourth dimension magic had been employed to expand the interior to accommodate all the families. I suppose they weren't entirely bad after all.

"Right, let me do the talking," Jules said once we'd all climbed out of the car.

She pinned an ID to her jacket, and I moved to bar her way forward. I jabbed at the thing identifying her as a library attendant. "Since when have you been mucking about with this lot?"

She rolled her eyes. "Honestly, Morgan, sometimes I wonder if you pay attention to anyone but yourself. I mean this in the kindest way possible ... but I told you ages ago I'd gotten a side job at the library."

"I thought you meant in London."

"Just because you think they're a bunch of useless wankers doesn't mean I do." She leaned in. "They've got their uses."

I held up my hands in a gesture of surrender and moved to fall in line with her as we walked to the door. She flashed the badge to a uniformed officer at the front door.

"They're with me," she said, waving her hand to encompass the rest of us.

"Nature of your visit?" the officer asked in a gruff voice.

"Unless I'm mistaken, anyone with magic has a right to come here and access the facilities," I answered, stepping up so I was toe to toe with him. "My name is Morgan le Fey. Check your records and you'll see I've every right to be here."

He pulled up a tablet and tapped at the screen, glancing at Jules again and then back to me. "Yeah, all right."

"Thank you," Julayne said and held the door open. "And you said you didn't have any gumption," she added as I passed her.

The interior of the building was decorated with portraits of past Council members dating back at least one hundred years. Most of the photos in the entryway were black and white. I caught Gethin studying the tiny placards on some of the frames.

"This says this person's family has been on the Council since the year 1907, is that right?"

"Oh, yeah, it's all hereditary bullshit," I replied. "Until a family dies out, they're in control."

"So, like a monarchy then," he noted.

Damn it.

"Just because I'm technically in line to rule Camelot, doesn't mean I think it's the best way of doing things," I said and gestured to the staircase to our left. "Come on, the library is upstairs."

I marched up the stairs to the fourth floor. Whoever thought to put the library this far up clearly had better stamina than the common man or well, me. Jules brought up the rear of our quartet.

"Head to the archives in the back," she called.

The archives were restricted. Unless you had an ID to get in. *Jules, I could kiss you.* Jules must have been preparing for this eventuality. She'd known that one day I might need access to the restricted historical materials, and she'd positioned herself here as part of a contingency plan. The library was chilly in the evening air as we walked in. The lights overhead were dim. Although the lamps positioned on tables were vibrant, dotting the space much like will-o'-the-wisps, the lights directing us to where we needed to go.

Jules hurried ahead of me and tapped her badge on an electronic door pad when we reached the archives. She shouldered the heavy wooden door inward and led us through into the darkness. Waving her hand in the air triggered the overhead lights, flooding the space with a soft orange glow. I was about to ask her where to go when she made a beeline for a far table with a computer terminal.

"I thought we might have some sort of quest on our hands after you went off," she began. "So, I've been logging everything I can on references to Camelot since then."

"You're bloody brilliant, Jules."

"Silly as it sounds, believing your destiny came true gave me something to strive for. Nim never told you, but even after you stopped listening to the stories, I had insisted she keep telling me. I wanted to know everything I could. It's what made me interested in history ... in all of this stuff."

It was almost like the universe was positioning her at my side for a reason. Like a knight. No, that was silly, wasn't it? I pushed the thought from my mind and gestured to the computer. "What have you found so far?"

"Unsurprisingly, not a lot. A couple of vague references to fairies and wild magic, but nothing concrete. Enough to make the connection that there was another realm, but nothing specific to Camelot."

"What if you search for the Grail? I mean that's been a myth in this world for ages," I replied.

She logged onto the computer and typed in the word, 'Grail.' She pivoted in her seat and held out her hand toward Gethin. "Can I see that sketch?"

He hurriedly tugged the notepad from his pack and handed it over. She scanned it in and added it to her search of the archives. I held my breath as I watched the percentage of the search creep towards 100%.

Part of me expected the results to find nothing. Instead, what appeared to be a journal entry popped up. Julayne zoomed in on the handwritten bit of text that also showed a rudimentary drawing that oddly looked enough like Gethin's sketch to be something. I was surprised I was able to read the cramped script.

I, Gaius de Byrne, Knight to His Majesty King Malachi of the realm of Albion, have pledged to remain and protect the blessed chalice from our foes. It is my solemn duty to guard it with my last breath.

I pointed to the word Albion on the screen. "That's got to be a veiled Camelot reference. Do we have a sense of how old this is?"

"Best guess looks to be about eight hundred years ago," Julayne answered, gesturing to a tiny note showing the age of the actual document based on carbon dating.

I turned to Emerys to ask if she recognized any of the names and saw a look of sadness and heartache etched into her usually stoic features. "You know something."

She swallowed, as if to find her voice. "I knew Gaius and his brother Wendell. They were honorable men." She dabbed at tears in her eyes. "I had thought they perished on a quest they undertook centuries ago for their liege."

"Who was their liege?" I pressed.

"They served King Malachi Pendragon, your ancestor ... and my husband."

CHAPTER
TEN

What? I couldn't have heard her right. I stared at Emerys in silence, trying to force my brain to accept the words she'd spoken.

"No, that can't be true," I blurted.

"I assure you it is," she replied. Even the way she straightened suggested the weight of the confession had lifted from her.

"But that means …" I began and she nodded.

"That I, too, am your ancestor." She offered a small smile. "Did you not wonder why I took such a keen interest in you? Why I spent so long finding a way to get to you and bring you home?"

"Sure, but I didn't think it wa-was because you were literally my ancestor," I answered, shaking my head. I spun to face Gethin. "Did you know any of this?"

He pushed his glasses up his nose and shook his head. "No. I swear. I mean, I knew she was long-lived and had some sort of special relationship to the royal family, but to be part of it, that's news to me."

"So, how come you're still here and everyone else is dead?" Jules interjected.

Emerys' fingers plucked the chain from around her neck, revealing the tiny gold dragon with its diamond at the center. "I was called to Camelot for a purpose. For many years I did not understand that purpose. It was not until my dear Malachi had passed that I was gifted with the magic to keep me young. And it was not until your birth I understood that I would be needed to protect my kingdom once more."

"Wait ... You had plenty of chances to tell me this when we first met," I yelled, anger increasing the volume of my voice. "You didn't think that information might help me trust you?"

"I am truly sorry for keeping it from you, Morgan," she answered, not meeting my gaze.

"Does my mother know who you really are?"

"She knows I hold a revered position in the

court, but it has been centuries since my descendants knew the truth of my identity." Again, that same hint of sadness at hearing Gaius' name washed over her face. "I never believed my kin would know me for who I truly am again."

I sunk into one of the chairs near the computer where Julayne still sat. This was too much. And yet, it made sense in a strange way. I couldn't really expect some all-powerful stranger to give a shit about my life. But a blood relation, no matter how far back she went, was another matter altogether.

"You said you were called to Camelot and that you passed through the barrier to get there. That means you're not really from there. You came from this world?" I posed.

"Yes."

"But if I'm related to you, and you're from this world, how come my magic was always shit before now?"

"As I told you when we first met, your magic was not born of this realm. My magic, yes, but it has been so intertwined with Albion's power for so long that I have adapted. You were never meant to be raised in this place."

"Her magic's fixed now though, right?" Jules said, sounding hopeful.

"She's brilliant," Gethin gushed. "She even created a portal to get us here."

"I knew you had it in you, love," she said, giving me an affectionate punch in the arm.

Silence fell over our group, and I studied Emerys with the benefit of this new information. I recognized the slope of her nose and that we shared some of the same coloring. But the red hair must have been weeded out genetically over the centuries.

"Not that I want to cut this family reunion short, but we do have the Grail to find," Jules said after a beat.

Gethin moved to peer over her shoulder, pointing to a spot on the screen. "Does that look like the page is torn?"

I scooted my chair to be in line with Jules and leaned in close to see what he was talking about. He was right. The scanned-in entry appeared to have been part of a larger page. "Good eye, mate," I said.

I turned back to look at Emerys. "Would Gaius have actually stayed behind if he went on a quest with the king?"

"Times were different in those days. While I was Malachi's equal in magic, I was not privy to all of his duties with his knights. But if he had a good reason to request one of his knights remain behind, then yes, Gaius would have been first to volunteer."

"I know it's been a while, but you don't remember anything about him mentioning going off to secret away the Holy Grail?" I prodded.

Emerys closed her eyes and took several deep breaths. I felt more than saw her magic envelop her. The air around her rippled and the tiny gem on her pendant sparkled in the ambient light as she continued to hold tight to the necklace. When she opened her eyes all of the color had drained from her irises and the whites had overtaken her pupils.

"There was a quest Malachi undertook shortly after the birth of our daughter, Mathilda. He would not speak of where the quest would take him, but I recall a distinct sadness upon his return—"

"Is there any reason they'd want to leave the Grail here? Gaius' note says he had to protect the blessed chalice," I interrupted.

The color returned to Emerys' eyes and the rippling effect faded. "I wish I could recall."

"Hang on, I remember something," Gethin said, excitement infusing his tone. "When I was a kid, I was kind of obsessed with historical magical arti-facts. A long time ago, there was rumored to be a goblet forged by dragons and imbued with human magic. It was said to be immensely powerful and if it fell into the wrong hands, it could be disastrous."

"That sounds much like the stories we've got here about the Grail," I said. "And I don't need to imagine what sort of shit the Seelies could get up to with that kind of power."

"Is there a way to see if we can find more of this writing, or this journal?" Gethin directed us back to the screen.

"The name is pretty distinct so if there are any other references," Julayne answered, her fingers flying over the keyboard.

A historical reference populated the screen. It appeared to be some sort of ledger with dates. While I'd been able to make out Gaius' writings, I couldn't make heads nor tails of the ledger.

"Can anyone read this?" I asked.

No one answered for a long moment. Jules snapped a picture with her phone. "There's an internal reference. Come on."

She abandoned the computer and dove into the shelves that lined the far wall of the archives. She trailed her fingers along the spines of dusty-looking texts, past artfully folded maps, and unbound manuscripts to the very last row. Jules handed me her phone while she tugged a thick volume from the shelf. She flipped it open to the title page and I let out a gasp.

"Records for magical practitioners imprisoned in the Tower of London," I read aloud.

Jules propped the ledger against the edge of the shelf and gently turned the pages, periodically checking the image on her phone to find the right place. The text wasn't any more legible in person either. *Damn it.*

The bracelet on my left wrist warmed and the sapphire glowed a pale blue. As if it had a mind of its own and guided my hand toward the page. I didn't fight it as my finger trailed down the page Julayne had turned to. Slowly, the text beneath the pad of my finger glowed the same hue as the gem on my wrist. Somehow, the text shifted, becoming readable.

"Gaius de Byrne, imprisoned from 1297 to 1307 for the crimes of employing dark magics against the crown," I read aloud.

"Except he was serving a different crown," Gethin muttered.

It made me wonder what sort of magic would be considered dark magic back then. "He wouldn't have brought the Grail with him to prison. They'd have taken it off him before throwing him in the tower," I noted.

Jules set the book down and turned to Emerys. "You said he had a brother?"

"Yes, Wendell. I'd thought them both lost on the same quest. Perhaps they both remained behind to guard the Grail and only Gaius was apprehended," Emerys replied.

"So, the Grail probably isn't at the Tower, but maybe the rest of that note from Gaius is there," I suggested.

"Is this Tower a place we could enter? If it was used for imprisonment, would the common people normally be permitted to enter?" Emerys asked.

"They do guided tours," I answered. "It's not actually used for keeping people locked up anymore."

"Then I suppose we know where we're headed next," Jules said, closing the book and reshelving it.

It was too late to go there now. Instead, we'd have to catch the very first tour in the morning. The thought of trying to sneak in after-hours crossed my mind, but my magic still wasn't that honed, and I didn't need the four of us ending up in prison ourselves.

"We're going to need to crash somewhere

tonight," I announced as Jules led us to the archives' exit.

She fell into step beside me. "So, what's with the glowing bracelet?"

I paused before we reached the door, looking around and checking to ensure we didn't have any prying eyes. I still couldn't quite shake the thought that we had a tail all the way from Ireland. I called my magic to the surface and the taste of lime coated my tongue as I did my best to conceal us from any potential magical intrusion.

"Well, it turns out magic swords are real. And dragon magic is pretty bloody cool, because it can turn one into this."

I pressed my finger to the sapphire and a trickle of lime wafted off my skin. I took a step back as the bracelet unwound itself, twisting and reforming until I held Excalibur in my right hand.

"Holy shit!" Julayne breathed.

"Weird as it is to say, it feels like part of the reason my magic was such crap before was because I didn't have this to channel my power," I explained, returning the blade to its less conspicuous form.

"Magic is a weird and wondrous thing," Jules offered.

I dropped the concealment spell and pushed the

ache in my temples away. Stepping back into the regular part of the Council library was blinding. It took a minute for my eyes to adjust to the relative brightness of the space. As we headed down the stairs, I couldn't help but feel a sense of excitement wash over me. I was descended from a long line of magic practitioners who went on literal quests back in the day. This felt a little bit like I got to live their stories. Now I just had to hope I wasn't utter rubbish at putting the pieces together in my own quest.

THE FOUR OF us spent the night crammed into Julayne's flat. If anyone had followed us, they would expect us to end up back at mine and Nim's place. Plus, if Jules was going to come with us—and I had every confidence she would—she needed to pack. She and I squeezed in together on her bed while Gethin took the floor in the living room and Emerys curled up on the couch.

"I'm really glad you're coming with us," I whispered as the clock ticked over to five in the morning.

"You know I'd go wherever you do, Morgan. We're a package deal, remember?" Jules answered through a yawn.

"I wish you could have been there for the tournament. I got to fight an actual dragon," I said, rolling over to face her in the darkness.

"I bet you were magnificent," she praised.

"Yeah, I was pretty good," I agreed with a sheepish laugh.

"What do you think the Grail actually does?" she murmured.

"Something important enough that they wanted to keep it out of Seelie hands," I replied. "Maybe it grants immortality. Or it gives you a bigger army. Or it just makes everything taste like your favorite drink," I rambled. Chalices were basically cups and used for drinking after all.

"You'll be bringing it home too," she pointed out.

The gravity of her words hit me, and I sat up. "King Malachi hid it away in this world for a reason nearly a millennium ago. What if I'm not meant to bring it back?"

"Things would have changed since then. Maybe whatever threat he was worried about has passed?" she suggested.

"Seelies live a long fucking time, Jules. Something tells me someone out there remembers the Grail."

"Well, we just have to find it first," she noted, and pushed herself out of bed. "Come on, we've got a prison to search."

We roused Emerys and Gethin, and after a quick breakfast of coffee with cheap scones—the look on Gethin's face was priceless—we headed into the city. We bought tickets for the first hour the Tower opened. While a guided tour would have given us more coverage within a group setting, the guides were keen to keep an eye on their group members. We needed to be able to slip away if needed.

"How exactly do you think we're going to find where they held Gaius?" Gethin asked as he fell into step beside me and we queued to be let in.

"If we're meant to be here and find whatever he might have left behind, I have to believe that my magic is strong enough to lead us." I waved my left hand to show off the bracelet. "Excalibur helped translate the ledger's text. I'm hoping it will give me the assistance I need to find and get us into his cell."

I caught movement out of the corner of my eye and turned to see more people filling out the line behind us—clustered in little groups. That sense of being followed hit me again. Logically, I knew that my magic worked here. But I still doubted it would be enough to guide us to the Grail and keep any potential unwanted guests from following us.

"I can't help but feel like someone's followed us," I hissed in Gethin's ear.

Somehow, to his credit, Gethin remained calm. I turned slowly so he faced the back of the line of people. I watched him stretch out his right hand, splaying his fingers. He was searching for any hostile magic. A slow wave of magic washed over me, and I felt it relax the tension in my shoulders a bit. Something deep inside me recognized his magic as friendly and cataloged it away for later. I suspected my magic would do the same for Emerys and Jules, too.

Tiny beads of sweat prickled along his brow the longer we stood there. When he finally let out an exhale his cheeks were flushed from the effort. "I get the sense someone's watching us too, but I can't pinpoint who exactly."

Asking Jules or Emerys to do the same might tip off whoever was watching us that we knew they were spying. We would need to be careful as we proceeded. I motioned for Emerys and Jules to move closer.

"Someone's watching us. I can't tell who, but we're definitely not alone," I said in a low tone.

"Should we split up? If there's only one of them, they can't follow all of us," Jules suggested.

I shook my head, "No, we stick together for now. Emerys and Gethin don't know the city and I'm not going to put them in danger if I can help it."

"A wise decision," Emerys agreed.

Behind us the doors to the Tower opened and security began letting people in, checking bags and screening them for illicit contraband. We passed through security and into the first level of the Tower. Let the search begin.

ELEVEN

Stepping further into the Tower sent shivers down my spine. Even without the knowledge that these walls once held a practitioner from another realm, the Tower's residents were legendary. Jules, Gethin, and Emerys clustered close behind me as I accepted a couple of tourist guide brochures.

"So, any idea where they would have imprisoned Gaius?" Gethin asked in a hushed tone. I caught him casting furtive glances over his shoulder as a group of school children passed us by.

"It's not like they put occupants' names on cells," Jules retorted.

"No, but I suspect he was unique enough to get a

mention in here," I noted and held up the brochure. At least, I hoped he was notable enough.

"Excuse me, you're going to need to move along," a female attendant said. "You're clogging up the entrance."

"Sorry," I said, and we moved toward the stairs.

I flipped through the guide as we went, trying to find any mention of Gaius. Nothing about him in the first few pages—when he would have been imprisoned—but there were entire pages devoted to Mary Queen of Scots' stay prior to her death.

"They actually imprisoned another ruler?" Gethin scoffed.

"Mary was a threat to the British throne," I explained. "You've got Seelies, we had mad monarchs of our own."

"We'd never be that brazen," Gethin murmured.

"A foreign power tried to murder me at birth and installed his own son as a fake heir," I reminded him.

"Good point."

"Let's just take it floor by floor and hope something becomes obvious," I said and moved off the first landing.

"I think I found something," Jules said, holding

up the brochure she'd taken from me as we made our way up two more flights of stairs.

We moved off to the side as one of the tour groups passed. For a brief moment, I could swear one of the young girls stared at me as if she recognized me. I arched a brow at her. She blinked and turned her attention back to the tour guide lecturing them on the Tower's history.

"Did you feel that?" Gethin whispered in my ear.

"Feel what?"

"Magic. When those kids walked by. It wasn't strong, but it was there."

No I hadn't, but it could explain why we'd both felt power in the queue. We couldn't be the only ones interested in the magical prisoners the Tower boasted housing over the years. For all we knew, they were all kids with magic. The unease that had been tying itself in knots inside my gut loosened a little. Even still, I waited for the girl to disappear from view before giving Jules the go ahead to share what she'd found.

"There was a man dubbed Mad Man Byrne held for attempting to perform dark magic on the King. The guards gave him the moniker after he was observed holding conversations with apparitions that could not be seen by others."

"I wouldn't blame him for losing his mind in this place," I said. "Does it say if he was ever released?"

Julayne flipped through a few more pages. "Looks like eventually, after about ten years, the Crown decided to release him after an anonymous benefactor paid a hefty fee."

"He did not die within these walls." The relief in Emerys' tone was evident.

"Now we know who to ask for," I said and went in search of a staff member.

We had to climb two more flights before I found someone who looked like they worked here. "Excuse me," I said, drawing the young man's attention.

"Can I help you?" he replied as if on autopilot.

"Yes, we were hoping to see the cell where they held Mad Man Byrne," I said.

The attendant blinked, clearly surprised by the request. If I had to wager, I'd say he was expecting a question about where Mary Queen of Scots had been locked up. He cleared his throat, as if having to go through a mental catalog to recall the proper response. "One floor down. But why would you want to see his cell?"

"She's just really into the occult," Jules answered and dragged me away before he could ask more questions.

We retraced our steps to the floor below and stepped off the landing out of the flow of foot traffic. Our quartet stood there in silence, unsure of what our next step should be. Maybe it was time for a little magic.

I inhaled, drawing my magic close. There was a small part of me that sighed with relief every time I went to do a spell now in this world and it went right. The world's ambient magic perked up as I gathered my power around me, listening keenly to my intent and desire.

Show me the way.

I opened my eyes to find pale blue boot prints disappearing down the corridor. No one else appeared to take notice of them. I took off at a leisurely pace and my companions fell into a tight knot behind me. The footprints turned, vanishing into one of the cells on the right.

"I think this is it," I whispered.

"What now?" Jules asked, peering around my shoulder into the room. "I don't see anything that would suggest magic."

Maybe it was the fact I was still fueling the spell, but I could feel an odd energy emanating from the room. I could almost swear I picked up on the stench of unwashed bodies and human filth from within.

Behind us, I could hear prepubescent voices and I turned in time to see the earlier school group wandering free of their tour guide. That same young girl caught my eye again and this time she stopped walking as her peers disappeared.

"Keep up, please," her teacher called.

She hesitated before rejoining her group. There was definitely something off about that girl. I turned back to the empty cell and barely stifled a gasp as I saw a figure peering out the window.

"What drew you here?" Emerys' voice came from my left.

"Didn't you see the magic illuminating our way?"

She shook her head. "I think perhaps you ought to go inside. If this was indeed his cell, there may be a clue left behind only for you to find."

The world shifted around me as I crossed the threshold. I turned to find the cell door firmly locked behind me. I peered through the small slits between the bars, but the hustle and bustle of tours had vanished. *What the fuck just happened?*

"How have you come?" a deep male voice asked from behind me.

I spun to find a man in a simple tunic and trousers standing by the window. He looked only mildly concerned by my sudden appearance. He had a tanned complexion a few shades lighter than Taron and Talia.

"Please, tell me how you have come to be here?" he repeated.

"I promise I'll answer your question, but I need you to answer mine first. Are you Gaius de Byrne, Knight of Camelot, and comrade to King Malachi Pendragon?"

His demeanor shifted and any amicability he'd shown me vanished. He raised his hands. "How dare you speak those names. You have come to take what is not yours. I will not give it to thee."

"No, please, I'm King Malachi's descendant. I know it sounds mad, but truly I am," I said, holding my hands out in a placating gesture.

"Words a Seelie spy would speak to gain my trust," he spat.

"I am not a Seelie spy," I said, trying to find something that would prove my identity. I had no bloody clue what might convince him. I took a step to my left and the sunlight coming in from behind him struck the tiny sapphire keeping the bracelet around my wrist secure. I hadn't had time to ask Emerys for specifics on how the family came to be in possession of Excalibur, but if I was lucky then he knew about the sword's unique link to the Pendragon bloodline.

"If I were a spy, could I wield the King's sword?"

"The dragon-forged blade? Only a Pendragon by blood can lay hands on the sword," he answered.

I pressed my right forefinger to the sapphire and the blade reformed in my hand. I held it out for him to inspect. His brow furrowed and he ran a tentative hand over the blade.

"This blade has seen battle. It had been newly forged when we left. But I have not been parted from my King so long..."

"I am telling you the truth. I am his descendant. I am on a quest of my own, seeking the Grail you brought to this realm from Camelot."

He took a shuffling step back, as if he still didn't quite believe me. "His heirs would not seek it."

"I'm not interested in whatever it does. To be honest, I don't even know why I'm meant to find it. I just know that I am, because it's supposed to help me in some big battle against the Seelies." I laid the sword down on the ground between us and pressed my hands to his arm.

His skin shifted beneath my touch, turning rough and scaly. His eyes turned a pale shade of orange and when he bared his teeth, his human ones had turned razor sharp.

"You're a dragon," I rasped. Emerys could have mentioned that.

"What else would I be?" he replied through a mouthful of jagged edges.

"I don't know how else to prove to you that I'm not going to hurt you. I don't know how I've even managed to end up here. One minute I was standing in the corridor with my friends and the next I walked in this cell to find you."

"I swore to the King, upon his wife's honor, I would keep it safe," he said. "And I have. The chalice is secreted away most safely."

"The Queen? You mean Emerys?" He nodded mutely. "She came with me. If I knew how to bring her here I would, but I don't have that sort of skill."

He stepped over the blade laying between us on the ground, his visage shifting back toward human. He tapped a finger against the lump under my shirt where the compass hung. "Show me what you hide, girl."

I resented being called girl, but I tugged the compass free of the fabric. He clasped it gently between his thumb and forefinger, tracing a tiny etching I hadn't noticed before in the surface. "This is Lord Eamon's work."

"Who?"

"A skilled craftsman and metal worker from my kingdom. I would know it, sure as I know my own magic. If he has gifted this to you, then you must speak the truth."

I didn't have the heart or the patience to tell him it came from a mystical cave. If he was willing to trust me now, I must use whatever time I had left to find out what he could tell me. "Then you know that I have a reason to seek the Grail."

He shook his head. "Words can be overheard. It is safer this way."

Before I could ask what he was talking about, I heard the jangle of keys in the corridor. I ducked out of sight, bending low to scoop up the sword. It molded itself back into the jewelry around my wrist.

"Mad aren't we, Byrne," one of the men on the other side of the heavy door called. "Talking to himself, railing on about spies."

The guards laughed before sliding a tray of food through the door and slamming it shut again. Gaius rushed forward and I thought he was making a beeline for the meager rations on the tray. Instead, he grabbed and shoved me at the closed door.

I braced for an impact that never came. Alternatively, I stumbled and bumped into Emerys and Jules. I blinked and the cell in front of me turned empty and clean. My head throbbed at the base of my skull.

"I—I need some air," I managed before taking off down the stairs two at a time.

I barreled past other patrons and tour groups, earning a few annoyed huffs as I shoved past people. I was only vaguely aware of Jules calling out apologies for my rush as she tried to keep pace with me. I skidded to a stop outside the Tower and past the queue still filled with people waiting for their tours.

"What happened up there?" Jules asked as she caught up to me.

"I was there with him," I said as Emerys and Gethin joined us. "I think I was the reason they called him Mad."

"Morgan, you think you time traveled?" Jules sounded incredulous.

"Maybe? I don't know exactly, but I talked to him. He thought I was a Seelie spy."

"He would have been distrustful of anyone appearing in a cell without announcement," Emerys agreed.

I tapped the compass. "He seemed to believe me

when he saw this. Said someone named Eamon made it." I pointed a finger at Emerys. "You could have told me he was a *dragon*."

"It did not seem relevant at the time. In Malachi's time, there was far more intermixing between the kingdoms. It was not uncommon to find a dragon knight serving a mortal king. Or even an Unseelie family living outside of their kingdom."

"What about the Seelies?"

"They would be the one constant throughout our history. Always at odds with the rest of the realm and thinking themselves above the rest."

I tucked the compass back beneath my shirt. "Anyway, just when I got him to trust me, he said he couldn't tell me anything … and then I was back here."

"You must have gotten something," Gethin insisted.

"Nothing. He said he hid the chalice and was keeping it safe, but gave me no clues where it might be. Even if he had, that was hundreds of years ago. For all we know he hid it somewhere that doesn't exist anymore, because it got bombed in the Blitz," I railed, starting to pace.

Out of habit, I shoved my hands into my pockets and stopped mid-step when I felt something in my pocket. I withdrew my right hand to find a folded piece of parchment—one edge clearly jagged and torn. I unfolded it to find a mess of gibberish I didn't recognize and symbols. Beside me, Jules pulled out her phone and brought up the image of the piece of paper with Gaius' name on it. I held up the piece. It certainly looked like it had come from the same parchment.

"It appears he did impart his wisdom on you after all," Emerys said.

I stowed it back in my pocket, suddenly feeling very exposed. Magic worked in mysterious ways. I definitely hadn't had the note when we entered the Tower. I could get lost in the weeds about how it had ended up in my possession later. But only when we were far from here and somewhere safe.

"It looked like some sort of map," Jules said, excitement creeping back into her voice.

A map we couldn't read and penned by a dragon who'd lived centuries ago. What could possibly go wrong?

CHAPTER

TWELVE

We made it half a block from the Tower before I stopped walking, realizing I had no sense of where we were heading or how the hell we were supposed to decipher Gaius' 800-year-old scribbles.

"We need to go somewhere private, but easily accessible," Jules suggested.

"Back to your flat?" Gethin offered, gesturing to me.

"No." That young girl's intense gaze flashed in my head again and for some reason I couldn't shake that there was something really off about her. "Jules is right, we need a place where we can get lost in the crowd."

151

I rubbed at the base of my skull, trying to think where we might be able to go. I glanced at Jules and we said, "Guildhall," in unison.

"It's perfect," Jules agreed.

"For those of us who have no idea what you're talking about, mind explaining?" Gethin asked.

"It was one of my Aunt Nim's favorite places. Come on. We can take the Tube."

I caught him mouth the word 'tube' to Emerys who offered him a confused shrug of her own as I set off down the road. Jules looped her arm through mine as we walked, and I couldn't help but rest my head on her shoulder.

"What was it like, meeting a dragon?" Jules asked in a conversational tone.

"Less exciting than the first time I met one," I answered with a snicker.

"I'm going to need more than that, missy," she chided.

"Turns out, the first time I met one, he walked out of a lake stark naked. It was glorious," I answered. "He was in human form at the time," I quickly clarified.

"I better get to meet this dragon someday."

"He's a prince, too," I added.

"Do I detect a royal romance?" she teased.

"No ... maybe. Oh, I don't know." I checked the street signs as we walked to Tower Hill Station on the District Line. "Anyway back to the Tower, like I said, I spent most of the time talking to Gaius, trying to convince him I was the Pendragon heir."

We walked on in silence for a moment before I asked, "What did it look like from where you were standing?"

"You went in and just sort of froze for a bit. Then, you stumbled backwards, and we left."

"You couldn't hear me talking to him at all?"

"Nope."

Her description felt like it gave more credence to the fact I'd somehow time traveled. Clearly, I was the reason Gaius had earned his Mad moniker amongst the Tower guards. We reached the station and set about getting us all through and onto the train.

Thankfully, the trip was a brief three stops to Mansion House. I studied Gethin as he took in every sight and sound of the city. I extricated myself from Jules' arm to walk beside him as we traversed the rest of the trip to Guildhall Library.

"I've been a terrible tour guide, I'm sorry," I said.

"You're a little busy questing," he reminded me. "I'm just grateful to be along for the ride."

"Well, where we're headed is one of the best places to learn about London's history. My Aunt Nim loved going there, especially in summer when school was out. She always insisted that my education not stop just because classes were done."

I was beginning to wonder if her love of this place had stemmed from a desire to understand the place she'd chosen to make our home. She could have stayed in Ireland after crossing through the barrier. Yet she chose London, all the way across the channel to raise me.

"I wish I could have met her," he said.

"Me, too."

"I know you said Gaius never really gave you a straight answer. But maybe there was something he did, a gesture or mannerism, that might have been a clue?"

"I wasn't exactly paying attention to that sort of thing," I sighed as the library building loomed ahead of us.

"We could always take another trip down memory lane," he suggested.

Doing it in Camelot had been tiring enough. I

wasn't sure I trusted my magic for a repeat performance on this side of the barrier.

"Let's get inside," Jules called, leading the way.

We sequestered ourselves in a quiet corner amongst the shelves. It was only then that I felt safe enough to bring the scrap of parchment out again. I laid it on the table between us.

"It's written in an ancient dragon dialect," Gethin announced almost immediately.

"Please tell me you've studied ancient dragon dialects," I said.

"When I was younger, yes. But it's been a while since I've had to try translating anything. And I don't have my reference guides."

"Whatever you can decipher is more than what we've got now," I said, pushing the fragment in his direction. Jules darted out of view momentarily, returning with a pad and pen.

"There was something that stuck out to me in the guidebook from the Tower," I said in a hushed tone, pulling the brochure out and flipping to the page where Jules had found the entry on Gaius.

I studied the information, reading each line slowly to fully process the content. He'd been released after a decade, because a rich benefactor had paid a hefty fee to the Crown. It sounded like he would have remained imprisoned far longer if not for the contribution by this mysterious patron with deep pockets.

"Would Gaius have made any connections in his time in London before being imprisoned?" I addressed Emerys.

"If Malachi tasked him and Wendell with protecting the Grail in this realm, I would imagine they would have been instructed to blend in as best they could. That would have taken some level of trust with the locals."

"Clearly someone didn't trust him since he was locked up," I muttered. I doubted he'd actually tried to act against the King of England. But then again, he'd appeared rather paranoid during our brief encounter. Maybe he'd feared they were in the midst of Seelie spies and reacted poorly.

"If they were going to trust anyone, it would have been those they would have believed incorruptible by magical influence," Emerys continued. "Clergy perhaps. Or possibly mundanes."

I hated to tell her that being a member of the clergy didn't exempt someone from being corrupt, but I held my tongue. We needed answers, not arguments. It seemed far-fetched that a man of the cloth would have had sufficient funds to free Gaius with a large payout to the King.

"Do we know what happened to his brother? Could he have spent that decade amassing wealth to free Gaius?"

"They were incredibly close. I would not doubt Wendell would have done all he could to secure his brother's release."

"I mean it would make sense. Dragons and treasure," Jules noted offhandedly. When Emerys gave her a quizzical look, she added, "Doesn't everyone know that dragons love hoarding shiny objects and amassing treasures?"

"All stereotypes evolve from a small ember of truth," Emerys noted.

"Is there any way we could find references in here about Gaius' whereabouts after his stay in the Tower?" I interjected.

Part of me thought we might have better luck back at the Council headquarters, especially now we had Gaius' prison name to search with. But if he distrusted other practitioners and instead relied on the kindness of mundane strangers, he might have ended up in the annals of mortal history.

"I'll see what I can find," Jules said and logged onto the library's internet.

I turned my attention to Gethin. "Any luck?"

He set down the pen and looked at me over the top of his glasses. "It's remarkable how clear the penmanship is. It's like it was written yesterday."

"Fascinating as that fact is, I'm more interested if you can figure out what it says?"

"There are a few symbols I don't quite recognize, but I think I've got one of these sorted," he pointed to a swirling symbol. "This means refuge. And this symbol is repeated a few times. I think it's what they were using to represent the Grail."

"Okay, so he stashed it in a refuge. Helpful," I groaned.

"Like I told you, I don't have my translation guides and it's been years since I've had to do any proper translating. I did notice something else, though."

I waited for him to explain, but he stayed quiet. "Well, what is it?"

"It might be nothing, but I think the people who wrote the two parts of this note were different people."

"I don't follow."

"The part that was written in English tilts a bit to the right, so probably written by someone who is right-handed. But parts of the map tilt the opposite direction."

"Could it just be that the two languages require different ways of writing?"

"Perhaps, but I think we're looking at two different scribes."

"So what, you think that Gaius didn't draw the map?"

"It's possible. And even if he did, why would he have penned the initial part in the first place? Why confess to being a knight of Camelot?"

"Maybe they tortured it out of him?" I answered with a shrug.

"Perhaps the more pressing question is why he held the map on his person, whether others could decipher it or not. Surely the guards would have searched him," Emerys interjected.

"Yeah, but I doubt they'd have denied him access to a priest if he asked," Jules said, looking up from her phone. "Looks like there was a Brother Jericho who was said to have left his wealthy family to follow his faith. He found Gaius' plight interesting and after a decade, managed to secure Gaius' freedom."

"Any idea where they might have gone after they freed him?"

"Looks like he was associated with a place called Lesnes Abbey," she replied. "But it shut down in the 1500s. It's a ruin now."

I plucked the phone from Julayne's hand and studied the images she'd found of the abbey. If someone else had written the map for Gaius to follow, they'd have to use markers he'd recognize at the time. I managed to find an image of the Lesnes Abbey in its prime and compared it to the symbols Gethin didn't recognize next to the one he'd identified as signifying refuge. It wasn't an exact match, but it was close. "I think you're both on to something. Someone must have passed him the map ahead of his release, so he'd know where to look later and for him to know that the Grail was safe. And if Wendell was still out there, and they were as close as you say, maybe he found this Brother Jericho. And he convinced him to take up his brother's cause."

"Jericho wouldn't have needed to know what the map said, he'd just need to know where to take Gaius when he was released," Julayne agreed. "And who would deny a man entry to a house of worship, especially if he claimed he was seeking penance and sanctuary."

"This all sounds good in theory, but Julayne just said this place is in ruins now," Gethin pointed out.

"Just because it's in ruins doesn't mean we can't learn from it. Who knows, maybe Morgan will time travel or get another vision," Jules said.

"Gethin was right about something else, it's possible I missed some other clue while I was talking with Gaius."

"I know you're worried about it, but I think you can do the memory spell again. Your power seems to be working just fine here," Gethin nudged.

"Using the memory spell too frequently can have deleterious effects on one's psyche," Emerys warned.

"What does the spell require?" Jules asked.

"It isn't hard to do exactly, just draining."

"What if you had a magic boost? I could give you some extra power just so you didn't have to rely on your own so much."

"It's worth a shot."

I scooted around the table, so we sat side by side and grasped her hands. I pictured the cell as I had seen it when I'd crossed the threshold and concentrated on projecting it so Jules and the others could see it, too.

The library disappeared, replaced by the rough

stone of the cell. The sunlight streaming through the window hit me in the eyes and I had to blink black spots from my vision. The image faltered as the trip down memory lane pulled on my magical reserves. The comforting feel of Jules' magic bumped against mine, as if to say 'I'm here, let me in.' I tightened my grip on her hand and urged my own power to accept the assistance.

Gaius materialized in front of us. I didn't need words to know that Jules could see him, too. We watched in silence as Gaius conversed with the memory version of me. I tried to pay attention to his hands, and the way he held himself for clues that might have been hidden during our first encounter. Nothing stuck out though.

"Did you see that?" Jules asked. She waved a hand and the moment froze, then grew bigger as she took control of the spell to zoom in.

"See what?" I tried to see what had caught her attention. She jabbed a finger at the compass around my neck. "It's just the compass. It's what led us back here."

"No, did you see what it did when he touched it?"

"Clearly not," I muttered.

I willed the memory to rewind and even

managed to get it to play at half speed. I focused on the object around my neck. His hands when he touched the compass were still covered in scales and claws. Except when they brushed the metal, something sparked, tiny designs flared to life for a brief moment.

"It looked like the symbols from the map, but that shouldn't be possible," I murmured.

"You're following clues left by a dragon centuries ago. Anything's possible."

Instinctively, my left hand reached up to find the compass lying against my breastbone beneath the fabric of my shirt. The object had brought me back home to Jules and to London. I had to trust that it would lead us to where we were meant to go next.

"We follow the compass," I announced to the people seated around the table as the memory faded. "And if it seems to be leading us to the Lesnes Abbey, then that's our next stop."

"I'll keep trying to decipher the rest of the map to see if it gives us any other clues," Gethin said, stowing his notes and the parchment piece in his pack.

With any luck, my magic would make things clear when we arrived at the abbey. As we left the library behind, the sense of being watched washed over me again. Maybe heading straight to the abbey wasn't the best course of action. I had to remind myself that soldiers had come through the barrier and nearly snuffed out my life once before. We had been careful on our exit from Albion, but there was every chance that King Uther had spies monitoring the barrier. We needed to be smarter about covering our tracks. We had a tail to lose.

THIRTEEN

Losing the tail turned out to be harder than I'd anticipated and not because I was bad at it either. The moment I started going any direction that wouldn't set us on the path to the abbey, the compass grew scalding hot against my skin. I finally tugged it over my head and held it as far from my body as I could.

"Morgan, what's going on?" Jules asked, taking the compass from me.

"I am almost certain we were being followed at the Tower. I was trying to lose whoever it was, but this damn thing won't let me."

"Is that even possible? This compass has that sort of power?"

"Dragon magic is immensely powerful. Something to do with the fact they've been around for thousands of years," Gethin offered.

I watched as Jules slid the compass over her head and stowed it beneath her shirt. "Maybe it will settle down if it's not with you?"

It was worth a shot. Besides, the time was heading toward lunch and my stomach gurgled with a reminder that surely people on quests were meant to eat and keep up their strength. I took a few steps in the opposite direction the compass had been leading us and kept my eye on Julayne. She followed me and to my surprise it didn't pull her back the way we'd been going. This just might work after all.

"So, if we aren't heading directly to the abbey, where are we going?" Gethin asked.

"Lunch." I wrapped my arm around his shoulders. "It's time you enjoyed some proper London food."

We ended up at a small pub about half a mile's walk from the Tower of London. We crowded around a table outside where I could sit with my back to the restaurant and people watch. Every child that walked past set my nerves on edge. I was vaguely aware of Jules ordering four plates of fish and chips.

"Okay, this is better than it has any right to be just looking at it," Gethin said, drawing me back to our group around the table.

"Yeah, that sounds about right for most British food," Jules agreed, tossing a chip into her mouth and munching. Our gazes met and she reached across the table, squeezing my right hand tight. "Everything's going to be fine."

"I just can't shake the feeling someone's following us."

"Could the Queen have sent someone, just to ensure we were safe?" Gethin asked between bites of breaded fish.

"That is not in Ingrid's nature," Emerys replied. "Or at least, it did not used to be. It would contradict her stated desire to remain ignorant of your whereabouts. If there is in fact a spy trailing us, I must believe it is Uther's doing."

"I didn't see anyone suspicious at the Tower," Jules said.

"There was this girl in one of the school tour groups. I saw her at least three times. Something just felt off about her," I insisted.

"Have you seen her since we left the premises?" Emerys leaned forward, looking up and down the street.

"No. But what if Arthur wasn't the only one living a lie in Camelot? Someone had to know the truth and help him. Someone could have been sent along to keep tabs on me for all we know."

"We're being careful," Jules said in a reassuring tone. If someone really was watching us, they'd assume our next move would happen now. So, let's throw them off and go tonight after dark."

"Jules, you're suggesting we break into a historical site?" I balked.

"Can you really break into anything if its already in ruins?"

"Yes," Gethin and I replied in unison.

"It may not be legal, but it would help obscure our intentions." Emerys gave Jules an approving nod.

"I have spent the better part of my adult life avoiding brushes with the law thank you very much." I wasn't keen to start a life of crime now.

"We need to go to the abbey. We also need to lose this tail. Going at night would throw them off. And it isn't like you'd be going alone. We've four very magical people. Between us, we should be able to manage to stay hidden," Jules said, taking a prolonged sip from her coffee mug.

I hated this plan. Sure, I wanted to be rid of any

prying eyes and ears, but risking our freedom felt like a foolish way to do it. Still, I couldn't bring myself to argue with them. I was still reeling from my little jaunt into the past. I wish I could have asked Gaius more questions about the realm he'd left behind. Why would he have volunteered to stay behind and risk his own life for the Grail? Was it really that special?

"What if we look him up?" Gethin blurted, disrupting my internal turmoil.

"Look who up?"

"Gaius," he said flatly, as if it should have been the most obvious thing in the world.

"You don't seriously think he's still around," I scoffed.

"He did say dragons have been around for a really long time," Jules pointed out.

"So what, we just look him up in the phone book?" Jules offered a shrug in response. "Even if we could, he probably changed his name every few decades to keep himself hidden. I would have if I were him."

"It is an avenue worth pursuing," Emerys noted.

"Probably safer to do research from the flat," I sighed. At least we would have secure Wi-Fi. And it might give the impression we were just out sight-seeing with friends for the day.

By NIGHTFALL, I was practically crawling out of my skin in anticipation. Gethin and Jules' internet searches for Gaius had come up empty. I couldn't help pacing the length of the kitchen as we waited for the sky to turn from a hazy purple to a deep navy.

"We shouldn't drive," I announced as my phone read nearly seven o'clock.

"Most of the trains won't be running now," Jules reminded me. "How else do you expect us to get there?"

"We can portal in. I've done it before. It's how we got from Liverpool to your flat."

"That nearly wiped you out," Gethin interjected. "No offense."

I looked at Emerys. "I'm not the only one who can do it."

"A portal in this instance would be the right choice. However, given the delicate nature of the portal magic I possess, I believe it would be stronger if we wove our magic together."

"Great. Let's get going then."

I shook out my hands, willing my nerves to subside as Emerys reached for me. We stood side by side in the kitchen and each raised a hand. For the briefest moment, I could see what she intended for us to do. As if she was sharing it with me so we could work in tandem.

"Remember, the portal must be a perfect circle," she said. Unlike last time when she'd coached me on this spell, her tone was soft and encouraging.

"Got it." I watched as she raised her hand. I matched her gesture move for move. Together we each traced an arc that connected to form the gateway to our destination.

I caught a glimpse of the world inside our portal, but it looked inky and undefined. I wouldn't want to walk through that. It was so unnerving that I took a step back.

"You need to envision your destination," Emerys said, gripping my other hand tight in hers.

"I've never been to this abbey. I've got no idea what it looks like," I replied as panic tightened my chest.

Jules rushed forward, holding up her phone and flipping through images she'd found online of the Lesnes Abbey. Somehow, she'd even found a few taken at dusk. I focused on the archway at the center of the structure, holding up the largest portion of wall. Power erupted from within me and when I looked through the portal again, it had filled with the night sky over the stone ruins of Lesnes Abbey.

"Holy, shit that worked!" I couldn't hide the surprise in my tone.

"I would advise moving quickly," Emerys urged.

Gethin shouldered his pack and offered Jules a hand as they stepped through the portal together. I looked at Emerys and tugged lightly on her hand. "Together then?"

"Together."

We leapt through and staggered forward until my hand brushed the rough stone of what was left of the abbey. I turned just in time to see the portal snap shut and out of existence.

"Okay, we're here. Now what are we supposed to do?"

Jules removed the compass chain from around her neck and handed it back. "I think this might have answers."

I accepted the chain and slid it back over my head. Holding it in my right hand, I watched as the tiny symbols glowed blue. Popping the top open, the tiny needle pointed straight ahead of us. I took a moment to take in the abbey ruins shrouded in darkness.

"We should have brought torches," I mumbled.

Without realizing what I was doing, my hands moved in a quick circular motion—relying on muscle memory from the tournament—and a greenish-yellow orb solidified between my fingers. I tossed it overhead to light our way.

"You picked up some neat tricks while you were away," Jules complimented.

"I just wish I knew what we were meant to find here." I continued to follow the compass as it veered vaguely to the left. "Even if Gaius had been brought here after his release, this place hasn't been a functioning abbey for like five hundred years."

"Look at you, doing research," Jules teased.

"I pick up books now and then," I said with a smirk. "And it looks like most of the place is gone anyway. There's just a few walls left now."

"I bet it was beautiful in its prime," Gethin said.

"I can sense the power that had graced this place," Emerys said, trailing her fingers along the interior of the wall as we walked. "They may not have been men of magic, but faith carries a power all its own."

I turned my attention back to the compass. It

was pointing straight again which made no sense. That way took me into the middle of a grassy space. "Come on, Gaius. What are you trying to show me?"

I stopped moving and tried to picture Gaius in my mind walking through the halls of this place. What could he have hidden away all those centuries ago that might give me a clue to finding the Grail now?

'Seek me, blood of my liege.'

His voice floated on the gentle evening breeze and when I opened my eyes, the compass burned bright, lighting up like a beacon. The light it cast shone on a row of bricks at the far end of the wall where a small portion of the adjoining structure still remained intact. As we passed by a window, I could swear I saw a light in the distance coming from the woods. I froze and watched as the light bobbed in midair, growing closer. Someone had found us.

"Get down," I hissed gesturing for everyone to stay low.

"Lawmen?" Gethin whispered.

I shook my head. "Couldn't tell. But someone is coming this way."

Our time was running out to find whatever Gaius had left for me to find. The compass and the orb that hung overhead still illuminated the bricks about a hand's reach from where I crouched. I hated the idea of defiling a historic landmark, but the future of Camelot depended on me uncovering what lay beneath those bricks.

I ran my finger along the mortar, hoping to find a crack big enough to let me wedge one stone free. Of course, they were sealed up tight. But in the bluish glow from the compass, I could see that the mortar in the area directly in front of me was far less aged than the stones around it.

"Anyone bring a chisel?"

No one answered. Digging at it with my hands would be pointless and I wasn't entirely confident, I knew how to use magic to free the stones without damaging the rest of the wall. I rested my forehead against the cool stone and the compass brushed the brick at chest height. The runes on the metal flared even brighter and when I looked down tiny depressions in the stonework appeared. I bent down to study the new marks on the wall to find they mirrored the ones on the compass.

"What is it?" Jules whispered.

"I'm not sure yet," I murmured. I brushed the pad of my thumb along the surface of the compass to find that the runes had become raised. Just enough the locket might fit into the newly revealed grooves in the wall. *Like a key.*

Oh, you brilliant bloody dragon!

I positioned the compass to line up with the grooves in the brick and pressed it as gently as I could while still ensuring contact between the metal and stone wall. I heard an audible click and the mortar around the brick crumbled, allowing just enough pace around it for me to wedge my fingers in and work the brick free.

I tugged it out of the wall, sticking my hand into the crevice before I thought better of it. I felt around until my fingers brushed something grimy, but flat and slender. I removed my hand to find an envelope with something written in the dragon dialect.

"Any idea what it says?" I held it up to Gethin in the light of the compass.

"If I remember my phonetic alphabet correctly it says M-O-R-G-A-N." He gave a soft strangled sound. "... it's got your name on it."

I turned the envelope over and undid the flap, revealing a slip of paper that looked at least fifty years old—colored with age—along with a photograph of two men, one of whom was clearly Gaius. The other man looked similar enough that they could have been brothers. *Wendell.* There was something scribbled on the back of the photograph, but I couldn't make it out even with the glow from the compass.

"It would appear that when you spoke to Gaius during his imprisonment, you did indeed travel to his era. He must have recalled you and knew what you sought," Emerys said, the wonder evident in her voice.

"I never told him my name. And this photo is maybe fifty years old at most. There's no way he could have hidden it in the abbey five hundred years ago."

"So, he came back to lay these breadcrumbs for you more recently," Jules remarked. "Brilliant."

It felt like such a long shot. How would he have intuited I'd have someone who could decipher the dragon text on the map? And yet, maybe it wasn't so off base. The compass had shared the same symbols. Perhaps it had worked in the same way Excalibur had allowed me to read the ledger of the Tower's prisoners. The compass could have let me decipher the directions to the abbey. There was so much about dragon magic and the magic from Albion in general I still didn't fully understand.

"Uh, Morgan, I think we should get out of here. We've got company!" Jules called just as a violent gust of wind ripped through the ruins and sent me flying sideways into the other wall. The collision knocked the air from my lungs and grey spots popped in my vision. I was getting really fucking tired of people throwing me into walls. Just as I tried to get to my feet, another blast slammed into me, temporarily turning the world and everything around me black as I fell unconscious.

FOURTEEN

Shouts roused me back to consciousness. When I opened my eyes, I saw two large blokes bearing down on Jules and Gethin while a third matched Emerys blow for blow at the far end of the ruins. Maybe it was the throbbing at the base of my skull, but I could swear at least one of them looked like the men Uther had sent to murder me and Nim. My ears rang with a painful high-pitched keening as I sat up. With it came a wave of nausea that was the farthest thing from regal and heroic. I felt momentarily helpless as I sat watching my friends take on these assailants. I tried a second time to sit up and the disorientation faded some. I raised my hand to brush hair from my face and felt paper crumple against my palm.

Somehow, I'd managed to keep hold of the photo and slip of paper. I shoved them down into my boot, discarding the envelope. At least this way they should be safe even if one of the men came for me.

The third time I tried to get to my feet succeeded and I balanced against the wall behind me until my vision cleared again.

"Get the fuck away from my friends!" I shouted, drawing a momentary glance from the man attacking Jules.

I reached toward my left wrist. Power had already wrapped around me like armor and maybe that was enough to trigger Excalibur's transformation. By the time I reached the melee I brandished a sword in my right hand. I swung at the nearest thug and to my surprise he spun, brandishing a blade of his own. The blades clashed and I went staggering backward, my left hand flailing to keep me upright.

"How'd they find us?" Gethin shouted as he barely dodged a fireball whizzing by his head.

"Fight now, questions later," Jules retorted as she made an effort to leap on the attacker's back.

As I regained my balance and thrust the blade toward my own assailant, I got a better look at him.

It was indeed the man who'd tried to choke the life out of me the night Nim died.

"Getting your arse handed to you once wasn't enough? Figured you'd come back for round two?" I quipped.

He snarled, his lips curling up over his teeth. "Fixing a mistake I made. I will not be denied again."

"Newsflash, dickwad, I've got a lot more power now," I taunted.

"I see no proof of that."

I realized the orb I'd created to light our way still hung in the air. I reached up with my free hand, willed it to burn white hot, and directed it at his torso. The greenish ambiance turned a blinding orange as it hurtled toward his chest. He held up his sword to block the flames, but some slipped past, singing his clothes to reveal a metal breastplate beneath.

"Children's magic tricks," he scoffed.

Was he trying to piss me off on purpose? I flashed back to the assault at the flat. He'd been almost resigned to the fact he had to kill me. This man was far more brazen, callous even.

"You felt bad about having to kill me before. I remember you showed remorse. What happened?"

My question caught him off guard. While I

would have liked to know the answer, I used the momentary distraction to switch Excalibur to my left hand and land a punch to his angular jaw. In hindsight, it might have been a better idea to magically punch him rather than use my actual hand. My hand ached and I'd broken the skin on several knuckles from the impact.

He recovered faster than I would have anticipated and spat a bit of blood into the grass. "You were feeble, powerless before. You were worthless. That's why I felt sorry for having to kill you," he said, his lips stained crimson with fresh blood.

"Nah, you weren't this much of a dick last time," I argued foolishly as I shook out the pain from my right hand. "I think you're showing off for your mates. Or your boss ripped you a new one."

Anger flashed across his face, contorting his angular features. It only made him look that much more savage and vicious. In that moment I believed every part of him was razor sharp and could have shredded my flesh if I got too close.

"Oh, that's it," I said with a laugh. "You had to go slinking back to Uther and admit you couldn't even kill some powerless woman. Bet that went over well."

"You know nothing of our king," he spat.

"I know he tried to murder an innocent newborn all because he's fucking crazy and abandoned his own kid in someone else's land for thirty years. All because he thought it might one day get him more power. Dad of the Year that one."

He recovered the blade he'd produced before and came at me, slashing wildly in front of him. There was no reason I should have been able to defend against his attacks. I wasn't a swordswoman. Yet, at every blow, Excalibur moved to block the advance, pushing my opponent back step by step until he was backed against the wall.

"Hate to tell you but you're going to have to go crawling back to him again, because I'm not going to let you hurt me or my friends."

In my peripheral vision, I spotted the brute Gethin and Jules had been tangling with as he slammed a foot into Gethin's solar plexus, knocking him flat on his back. He'd lost his glasses some-where in the brawl and he sported a cut under one of his eyes. I waited for him to get up, but he laid still. I could see his chest rising and falling so if anything, he'd just been knocked out.

The sky lit up with plumes of turquoise smoke as Emerys and her adversary traded spells at such speed I couldn't even tell where one spell ended and the other began. But their spell battle lit up the sky, a beacon to let anyone else know where we were. Magical fights are not the best move for a covert mission.

My own adversary recovered from being backed into the wall and tossed his sword aside. Instead, he lunged for me around the middle. Somehow, I avoided his grasp. When I looked down, I found the blade in my hand slick with blood. For a split second I feared I'd run him through. But when I glanced his way, I saw I'd only managed to slice a thin gash along one of his arms.

"Get away from him!" Jules bellowed as the third Seelie advanced on the still prone Gethin on the grass. She waved her hands in an intricate gesture and the grass leapt up to twine around his feet, slowing his progress.

He started to rip the makeshift bindings with his hands, freeing himself in moments. Jules mimed tying a series of knots and the grass obeyed her command, tightening. Still, it wasn't enough to hold him.

"Their magic is tied to nature," I shouted at Jules, but she didn't acknowledge hearing me.

Leaving my soldier to bleed, I raced to Gethin's defense. I swung Excalibur toward the brute's midsection, hoping to distract him from dismantling Jules' magic. He dodged, pulling free from the roots in one fluid motion and I narrowly avoided slicing Jules in half. It gave the thug just enough time to rip Gethin's pack from his shoulder, rummaging through the contents.

"No!" I shouted and threw my hand out.

I wasn't sure what I expected to happen. In my head, I envisioned him still as a statue. In reality, his limbs appeared to grow stiff, but a violet streak of energy from Emery's fight interrupted the spell. It threw him backward, pack still in hand as he landed on the grass. The thug recovered his wits far too quickly, returning to his task.

I could only stand frozen as he tossed the pack aside, having found whatever he was looking for. He secreted it away before I got a good look at what he'd taken. But there were only a few things of value to this quest in Gethin's possession. I was about to take another swing at the bastard when a high-pitched whistle echoed through the air. I bent double, sure my eardrums were about to rupture. Covering my ears only seemed to make the sound echo more painfully in my skull. Jules suffered a similar reaction, gritting her teeth in pain as she spun wildly in search of its source. I could make out a hazy green aura around Emerys that appeared to protect her from the sound. Too late, she began to send it cascading our way. All three Seelies stopped mid-motion. The one who'd been facing off with Emerys looked annoyed.

"What's going on there!" a male voice called out from beyond the ruins. It was only thanks to Emerys' barrier I was able to make out the man's words.

The Seelie soldiers vanished withaudible pops, leaving the four of us in the center of the ruins in various states of disarray. I did my best to hastily wipe the blood off Excalibur's blade in the grass before it returned to bracelet form.

"Morgan, it's the police," Jules said, her voice barely above a whisper as she pressed herself just below the bottom of the nearby window.

We couldn't get caught. "Bobbies really? Help me get him up," I said, not caring whether Emerys or Jules came to my aid.

Gethin was still unconscious. I didn't have any definitive proof that going through a portal while not fully aware of one's surroundings would do any lasting damage. However, I wasn't keen to find out while trying to evade the law.

"Sorry about this, mate," I said and slapped him across the face.

It did nothing to rouse him. My heart dropped into my stomach. I leaned in close, holding my breath until I was absolutely certain I'd heard and felt his heartbeat. Hitting him again wasn't the answer and shaking him felt unwise, too. I did the only other thing that came to mind. I kissed him hard on the mouth.

His steady breathing turned into a gasp of surprise and his eyes flew open. Our gazes met and the world stopped for a beat. I pulled away after a moment more and straightened.

"Had to be done," I announced.

"Uh, right," Gethin mumbled as he went in search of his glasses.

I peered through the closest opening to me. I could just make out uniforms and badges as the sweeping beams of police torches moved from side to side. Two officers approached based on the bouncing lights. From the shouting earlier I knew one was male. Since I'd extinguished the orb of light, I could only guess his partner's gender.

"We need to go," Jules reminded me.

Not that I'd forgotten. I turned to Emerys,

extending my hand. But even in the moonlight I could see her skin had gone pale and her shoulders drooped with exhaustion. Fighting off the third Seelie had taken more out of her than I would have expected. It was up to me to get us back to the flat before they found us.

You can do this, Morgan.

I blew out a breath and raised my hands, tracing the circumference of a circle in midair. The edges of the spell sparkled and sputtered as I poured as much power as I could muster into it. I tried to picture the kitchen in the flat I'd shared with my Aunt Nim. The image within the spell's boundary flickered, finally solidifying into the image I'd intended.

"You're going to need to move quick. I don't know how long I can hold this," I said, already feeling the strain of sustaining the magic.

The torch beams grew closer and spread out as the police closed in. Beads of sweat prickled along the nape of my neck and bloomed beneath my arms. Gethin stumbled through first. I watched him skid to a halt against the sink.

"Jules, go," I said.

"You'll be right behind me, yeah?"

"Always," I answered.

She leapt through far more gracefully than Gethin and landed squarely on the tile floor. I nodded for Emerys to pass through the barrier, but her gaze was fixed on a point over my right shoulder. I turned my head just enough to see that we were out of time. Even if she made it through in the next twenty seconds, there would be no way I'd get through without them seeing something. And while magic wasn't exactly a secret it didn't mean these particular officers were privy to the details. I didn't need mundane cops seeing me vanish into thin air and having a coronary.

Time slowed as I lowered my hands. I pulled back on my magic, willing it to recede into my body and tamp down. The portal in front of me winked out of existence between one breath and the next. The beams of light rounded the wall and the two officers—the second now confirmed as a woman—stepped around the wall. The torch light temporarily blinded me.

"Stop right there," the male officer ordered.

"We're not moving," I called.

"Hands up," the female officer barked.

I held my hands high, praying that Emerys would follow suit. My vision cleared a moment later and the female officer approached, a pair of cuffs dangling from her hand. I instantly distrusted her. The smug look on her face just rubbed me the wrong way. But I'd expended enough magic today that I wasn't going to be able to tell whether she was a magical or mundane threat.

"You two are trespassing on government property," she said. There was a note of glee in her tone. This was probably the most action she'd seen on the night shift in ages.

I bit back a snarky retort and kept silent. She was rougher than she needed to be as she yanked my hands behind me and secured the cuffs around my wrists. Within the span of five minutes, they marched us to their waiting vehicle and crammed us into the back.

Well, shit.

FIFTEEN

It felt as though we'd been driving for ages. The female officer drove, and I caught glimpses of the male officer's eyes as he glanced at us in the rearview mirror. He'd been far gentler with Emerys when he'd cuffed her than his partner was with me.

"Want to tell us why you two were coming to blows in a historic site in the middle of the night?" His tone was more curious than accusatory.

"We were not—" Emerys began, but I cut her off.

"It was a dare. We'd heard the Brotherhood that used to reside there liked to hide things in the walls. Some friends of ours bet us two hundred pounds that we wouldn't go in after hours and see what we could find."

"Those rumors pan out?" I watched his reflection in the mirror and his eyebrows arched.

"Nah. Just a bunch of old stones. Nothing secreted away. Wasn't worth the money."

"Seems you two need some better mates," he noted.

"And the uh bloody knuckles?" He held his hand up to shoulder height and wiggled his fingers.

"Didn't think the plan through. She forgot a chisel. Stupid me tried to punch the bricks," I lied.

The clock on the dash read nearly half past ten by the time we pulled into the police station. I expected them to separate us and question us individually. Instead, they ushered us into lock-up, which was to my surprise empty. A bored man with a hooked nose and watery eyes sat at a nearby desk flipping through a newspaper.

"Ruthless Ruth actually bagged one?" he asked with mild interest as the female officer undid the cuffs around my wrists with more force than necessary. "Wonders never cease."

"Shut it, McDougal," she spat. "Caught these two trespassing on government property. Defaced it, too."

That was enough for McDougal to set his paper down. "These two?"

"Allegedly," I answered.

"Come on Franco, we've got paperwork to fill out," the female officer said, securing the cuffs back onto her belt.

Franco trailed after her, looking resigned to his evening of forms. I sunk onto one of the benches bolted to the wall and rested my head against the concrete slabs behind me.

"I told you this was a bad idea," I finally said, eyes closed. "I told you I couldn't afford to get caught."

"It was not my intention to be waylaid by assailants, nor that their magic would draw the local law."

"We could have gone in the morning, blended in with tourists," I hissed. "It would have been safer."

"If you must be upset with me, fine. Get your anger out. But we do not have time for such childish emotions."

"Childish?" I spat, my eyes snapping wide open to look at the woman who stood on the other side of the cell. "I told you it was dangerous, and you pushed to do it anyway." I cast a quick glance toward McDougal who'd gone back to reading his paper. "You may have come from this world, but that was a long fucking time ago. Things aren't the same way you left them."

"You are correct, they are not as I left them. But I have learned to live in the modern world and this place is not so different from Camelot."

"I think you spent too long without being around people," I muttered.

I began to pace, frustration bubbling to the surface. "Explain something to me. You're supposed to be this super powerful witch. I've seen you do epic shit, but fighting off that bloke tonight wore you out? How? What's going on?"

"He was more powerful than the two soldiers I dispatched upon my arrival here weeks ago. And my magic has adapted to Camelot. It is a strain to work it in this realm, much like you've experienced."

The way she didn't meet my gaze suggested there was more to the story. But in the time I had known her, and I'd admit it was a very short time, Emerys had never been an open book. It had taken three weeks for her to even tell me we were related. As that thought crossed my mind, the frustration ebbed, replaced by a helping of guilt. She'd come to teach and protect me on this search. And here I was yelling at her, because she wasn't magical enough? How hypocritical of me.

"Look, I'm sorry. I'm just panicking a little. We're stuck here overnight. And we have no idea if Jules and Gethin are okay. Or if they'll even be able to find us here."

"I have to trust that they will come for us," Emerys said softly.

"This almost felt like we were set up to lead the Seelies right to the abbey," I said, resuming my pacing.

"They should not have been able to track us given the way we arrived," Emerys agreed. "You said you felt we had been watched from the beginning. Could they have followed us to the library and over-heard our discussion about the abbey?"

"It's possible. But that still doesn't explain how they got there right after us. They couldn't have just gone and waited all day. There could have been other clues we were following."

"Then it stands to reason they trailed us from Camelot."

"I still don't get how though. We left from the castle and went straight to the forest."

"We are not the only ones who are aware of the barrier."

We weren't going to puzzle out how they'd found us at the abbey, not while sitting here in this damn cell. As I pivoted to begin tracing the grout in the floor, something poked my ankle and I let out a soft hiss of surprise. I bent down and tugged at my boot, finding the slip of paper and photograph I'd stashed there. Thankfully, Ruthless Ruth hadn't deemed it fitting to frisk me upon arrival. She'd forced me to turn over my phone, but she hadn't confiscated the compass or the papers I'd stowed.

I checked to ensure McDougall was still occupied with his newspaper before I settled back on the bench and gestured for Emerys to join me. She sat and we both turned as much as we could to block his view of the items I now held in my hand. Emerys took the photograph from me, and I saw her face fall with unshed tears sparkling in her eyes.

"Based on the uniforms it looks like World War II," I explained, realizing an instant later that she likely had no idea what I was talking about. "Basically about seventy years ago, there was a big war between us with our allies and some people who honestly would probably get on grand with the Seelies. There was a lot of devastation."

She tapped the man on the left in the medic uniform. "That is Wendell."

"Did he have any medical skills? Healing?"

"Basic training in how to treat field injuries, but

nothing beyond that. Dragons typically are not gifted with such magic."

"Well, it looks like he signed up to help wherever he could." I pointed to Gaius in a military uniform. "Looks like someone found a new crown to fight for. I'm not sure, but it looks like he could have been a pilot."

"One way to take back to the skies," Emerys murmured. "They both lived long after I thought them dead."

I turned the photograph over to find an address scrawled on the back in penmanship that looked similar to the note Gaius had penned all those centuries ago upon his imprisonment.

"It's an address." If I'd had my phone, I could have looked it up. We could have been one step closer to finding where Gaius was sending us next. "Which will have to wait until we get out of here."

"What is this?" She plucked the slip of paper from my hand.

In the light of the holding cell, I could see that it appeared to be a handwritten receipt. There was no header on it to identify a shop and given that it was in the same envelope with a seventy-year-old photograph, I didn't expect it to have a working telephone number either. The script was neater than the address on the back of the photo, but it still looked to be Gaius' penmanship.

Remit to holder:

Jericho spirits - 25 Nov

Wares of kings - valuation pending

Honor et Praesidium aeternum - upon request

"This makes no sense," I groaned.

"Was he not freed by a man called Jericho?" Emerys pointed out.

"Yeah. And we assumed if Gaius survived, he would have taken on other names as time passed. Maybe he took inspiration from the man who set him free?"

"What do you make of this?" she said, pointing to the number on the first line.

"Looks like a date. The twenty-fifth of November. But there's no year."

"What's this gibberish at the bottom here?" I pointed to the third line of text.

Emerys smiled. "Honor and protection eternal. It is on the coat of arms for the dragon royal family."

"So, he didn't forget where he came from?"

"Perhaps."

That left the middle line. The answer felt like it was staring us in the face. And yet, the late hour and the exertion from the scuffle with the Seelies had turned my brain to mush.

"Let's get some sleep. Maybe this will make more sense in the morning," I said, barely stifling a yawn.

"Yes. Get what rest you can."

I stowed the photo and slip of paper back in my boot before I tried to curl up on the bench. There wasn't enough space for both of us to lie down. I felt bad for taking up most of the room, but Emerys just sat there. She patted her lap, and I laid my head on her legs. She wound her fingers lightly through my loose locks of hair in a calming motion.

"It has been so long since I did this," Emerys whispered. "I can still recall nights spent with my dear Mathilda in my lap as a little girl. Before Malachi's passing."

"What was she like, your daughter?" I asked through another yawn.

"Fiery. Contrary, as I suppose most daughters are meant to be. But in her day, she resented me for not allowing her to take the throne when she thought she should. I knew she was not yet ready for the responsibility."

"Everyone thinks they know better than their

parents." It was getting harder to keep my eyes open.

"Yes, that is a truth that transcends the ages. But she did take her place as Queen, and she was magnificent. And I could finally step back into the shadows, advising my kin, keeping hold to them, but not so tight as to stifle their journeys."

In that moment I realized that she must have watched so many of her descendants die. "It must have been so lonely, seeing everyone you loved grow old and die."

"Yes, there was sadness as I lived on, but I also received the gift of sharing time with those I would not have otherwise."

"How'd you end up with that gift?"

Her fingers wound through my hair some more, brushing lightly in places against my scalp. "A tale for another night. Sleep now."

It didn't take long for the weight of the day to catch up with me, pressing me firmly into slumber.

"OI, LE FEY," a gruff voice called, jolting me awake. "Pendragon."

I sat up, a pain in my neck from the angle I'd

fallen asleep. Emerys was already standing as I got my bearings. I wiped the sleep from my eyes and scrambled to my feet to see Officer McDougall standing on the other side of the door, keys in hand.

"Looks like you're getting off easy," he said as he turned the key, releasing the lock and letting the door swing toward him.

"What?"

"Apparently, you've got a guardian angel looking out for you. No charges are being filed. You're getting off with a warning, this time. You can collect your belongings at the front desk."

"Right. Thanks, Officer." I darted past him out of the holding cell. "I promise you won't see us again!"

As Emerys and I left the holding area behind, I could swear I heard him say, "Seriously, le Fey, Pendragon. What a bunch of made-up nonsense."

Whether he believed our names or not, I was just grateful someone had managed to keep Ruthless Ruth off our case. The details of why there were no charges pressed piqued my curiosity. For a brief moment I thought about doubling back to ask Officer McHugh for details, but we needed to get out of here before anyone changed their minds..

Hopefully, Jules and Gethin had stayed put in the flat. We needed to get back to them and strategize our plan of attack. With any luck, maybe they'd managed to figure out how the Seelies had tracked us to the abbey.

We made our way to the front of the station and the desk sergeant handed over my phone in a clear baggie. He looked perplexed when Emerys assured him, she had no belongings to claim. I emptied the bag, handed it back to him, and hit the power button on my phone. But nothing happened.

Damn battery.

I turned back to the desk. "Sorry, would I be able to borrow your phone to make a call? We need a ride."

"Yeah, all right," he answered and turned the desk phone around so I could reach the keypad and receiver.

"Morgan!" Julayne's voice rang out before I could pick up the phone.

I pivoted toward the front door to find Jules and Gethin standing there. They looked like they'd had about as good of a night as we did. At least Gethin's injuries were far less noticeable now. I threw myself at my friends, holding tight to the pair of them. "Oh, thank God you're okay."

"This is the sixth station we've tried this morning. We just kept calling until someone finally told us you were here," Jules said in my ear. "I'm sorry we didn't get here sooner."

"Somehow we got lucky, and they aren't pressing charges," I said as I released my grip on the two of them and let them lead us out to the street.

"That would be us," Gethin said. "Julayne contacted the Council and convinced them to intervene on your behalf. She was very persuasive." The admiration was clear in his voice.

"They won't even see any damage when they go back there to check. Not that you really did much damage, but there was considerably more blood than I thought," Jules said brightly.

I didn't question whether that would risk more magic exposure in the long run. After all, I'd admitted to doing damage to the wall of the abbey. But I wasn't going to look this particular gift horse in the mouth. Whatever my hang-ups with the Council, in this instance they were definitely not as bad as Aunt Nim had made them out to be.

"We need to go somewhere busy and out in the open, where even if the Seelies find us, they won't be as inclined to attack us. We have a lot to talk about."

SIXTEEN

The moment we walked away from the station; my stomach gurgled a reminder that I hadn't eaten in ages. I spotted a café up the road and made a beeline for it. The rest of my party kept pace, and we managed to get a table in the back corner. Once seated the server stopped by with menus and a pot of coffee.

"Well, I know why we look like shit," I said once I'd poured my second cup of coffee. "Why do you two look like you haven't slept all night?"

"Because we spent most of the night trying to track you down," Gethin answered. "Like I said, the Council was instrumental in making sure you didn't get charged."

I looked at Julayne. "They really came through for me?"

"They don't necessarily believe you're heir to some mystical realm or anything, but I impressed upon them that you were someone who should be taken seriously. As soon as the portal closed behind us without you, I knew we didn't have a lot of time to act," she explained.

The server came back, pen poised over paper to take our orders. After a little menu shuffling, we'd placed our orders and the server left us in peace. I turned my attention back to Jules. "Do you have any idea how they found us?"

"They were tracking me," Gethin said, head hung low. "I should have realized something was off, but I didn't," He glanced over to Emerys, who to this point had remained silent save for ordering her meal. "I failed in my training."

"It is I who owe you an apology," Emerys replied. "I knew this journey would excite you. I spent much of our time together preparing you to work beside Morgan, but I did not take into consideration how much leaving Camelot behind would impact you."

"How did they track you?" I interjected.

He rummaged in his pack and pulled out a tiny pebble. It could have come from a million places. He set it on the table between us, glaring at the perfectly round object.

"I never would have noticed that," Julayne said, giving Gethin's shoulders a firm, supportive squeeze before continuing. "It's been neutralized now. At least we're mostly certain it has been."

"Another assist from the Council?" I barely hid my skepticism.

"Conrad," Jules answered.

I nearly spit my coffee across the table. "You two had an actual conversation?"

"We are adults, Morgan. We are perfectly capable of keeping things professional."

"Who is Conrad?" Emerys interjected.

"Julayne's ex-boyfriend," I noted. "Horrible break-up because he's a gutless wanker who cheated on her. For months after she dumped him, all they did was glare at each other whenever they crossed paths."

"I knew I didn't like him," Gethin muttered.

"Like I said, we're adults and far more mature than when that happened," Jules said, brushing her hair back over her shoulder.

"It was six months ago," I stated flatly.

"Anyway, it looks like Seelie magic. I've read about tracking stones like this. But the information we had in the archives in Camelot was a bit sparse on details." Gethin redirected the conversation.

"Can we use it to see where they are?" I picked up the tiny stone, turning it over in my palm.

"Seelie magic is far more temperamental than most," Emerys explained. "As you know, magic is shaped by intent. Seelies believe themselves superior to others and would never permit their magic to be so easily turned against them."

"Do we think they slipped this in at the Tower?" I set the stone back on the table.

I couldn't explain the strange vibe I got from the young girl on the tour. For all I knew, they'd offered her money to slip it into Gethin's bag while we were distracted. Or maybe one of the soldiers had used an illusion like Arthur had done?

"It's possible. It definitely would have given away the fact we'd gone to the abbey," Jules agreed. "And clearly they have transportation magic of their own."

I took my coffee cup and pressed it down as hard as I could on the stone, waiting to hear a soft crack. I ground it into the table just to be sure and swept it on the floor. "Now they definitely can't track us."

The server chose that moment to appear with our food. My stomach gave another audible growl as she set my plate in front of me. I caught Gethin eyeing his identical plate, digging in with vigor. Silence fell over the table as we occupied ourselves with the meal. Ten minutes later, I set my utensils down on my now empty plate and let out a soft contented sigh.

"The soldiers who accosted us took something from Gethin's pack," Emerys said, setting down her own coffee cup.

"They got my notes and the piece of parchment with the map from Gaius," Gethin admitted.

"Were you able to decipher any of the rest of it before they got their hands on it?" My voice came out sounding hopeful.

"No. I'm sorry, Morgan."

"Perhaps our discoveries will make up for it." Emerys nudged me in the ribs.

For a split second I wanted to ask what she meant, until it dawned on me. I shifted in my seat to pull the photo and slip of paper from my boot. I laid both on the table between us.

"This is Gaius and his brother," I explained.

"Looks like a few hundred years changes a man's willingness to serve a different crown," Gethin murmured.

"Looks like they were just trying to help the

people they'd chosen to live with," Jules countered. "Seems very honorable and noble of them. Besides, the Second World War was brutal here. Air raids, gas attacks, genocide."

"Helping those less fortunate is a quality Malachi admired in his knights. These two were no exception," Emerys confirmed.

I turned over the photo to reveal the address written on the back. "My phone's dead or I would have looked it up already."

Jules snatched the photo from the table and turned her attention to her phone. Meanwhile, Gethin studied the slip of paper. I watched his brow furrow as he mouthed the final line. He glanced at Emerys.

"That's the dragon kingdom's motto on their royal coat of arms, isn't it?"

"It appears I did not entirely fail in your training after all," she replied with a smile.

"Dragons aren't exactly known to speak in riddles," he said. "And this just looks like nonsense."

"I mean it's possible he's telling us to find an antique bottle of wine," I said. "I mean spirits are alcohol."

"Gaius knew even when I found him in the Tower that people were after the Grail. He was distrustful of me, too. I wouldn't blame him for writing this in some sort of code to ensure the right person found it and could decipher it," I said.

Not that I had any idea what the other pieces of the puzzle meant—a date with no year, a reference to a King's wares and its value pending. What the hell did that even mean? And did he just assume I knew what was on the royal coat of arms from a kingdom I'd technically visited one time. And unless he was psychic—which given our interaction I doubted—he would have no way of knowing that.

"Not to rain on anyone's parade, but I don't think you're going to like what I found," Jules interrupted.

She passed me her phone and the photo. I checked the address she'd entered against the writing on the photo before I scrolled down to show that the location was for a cemetery.

My stomach dropped and I regretted packing away an entire plate of food so quickly. A tinny ring filled my ears and my vision tunneled. All I could see was the image the internet search had revealed of a lone decrepit tombstone.

"This can't be right," I finally managed, pushing the phone back across the table to Julayne.

"You can see for yourself, I put it in exactly like it was written."

"Maybe he just hid another clue there?" Gethin offered.

Emerys leaned forward, studying the back of the photograph. "There is a sequence of numbers that I do not see there."

"I'm guessing we aren't going to figure it out just sitting here," Jules said, tossing a few bills on the table.

None of the rest of us moved. "For all we know, this same information was in what the Seelies stole from Gethin, and they've got dragon translation guides to help them figure it out. We can't assume they're a step behind now that we've cut off their ability to find us at will."

She was right. No matter how much I didn't want to face what awaited us at the cemetery, we didn't have a choice. Besides, that was where Gaius wanted us to go next.

IT WAS STRANGE, but I'd never been to a cemetery before. It had always just been my Aunt Nim and me and it wasn't like we'd lost anyone else close to us. I knew some people found them peaceful, but I couldn't shake the unsettled feeling that wrapped itself around me as we approached the wrought iron gates.

"Are you all right?" Gethin asked, falling into step beside me.

"Yeah, I'm fine. Just trying not to imagine what we're going to find among a bunch of corpses."

He nodded and then said, "You're not angry with me for letting them track us?"

"Why would I be mad? It wasn't your fault. We had a lot going on with the tournament and the announcement about who I was. It's understandable you might not have picked up on someone slipping that into your bag."

"I spent most of last night beating myself up for it."

"Well, not that you need it, but I give you permission to forgive yourself, mate. You didn't do anything wrong."

"Thanks." After a beat, he added, "I know it's not the best timing, but I just wanted to say that kiss was ..."

A lump formed in my throat as he trailed off. It had felt like the right thing to do in the moment, and it had in fact jolted him awake. But as I replayed the scene in my mind, a realization struck me. Upon first meeting Gethin, I'd noticed his charm. He was definitely attractive, sweet, and funny. Yet, when I'd kissed him, there hadn't been anything romantic in the gesture.

"I didn't know how else to get you conscious," I blurted.

"Oh." His cheeks turned pink in embarrassment, and he averted his gaze. "I was going to say it was nice, but felt sort of like kissing a relative."

Relief washed over me. "Exactly how I felt." I let out a laugh. "I was a little worried this conversation was going to be awkward."

"Don't get me wrong, I think you're beautiful and amazing. But I also have seen the way you are when you're around Taron. He's definitely more your type."

"Is he a bad boy?" Jules piped up.

"No," I scoffed with a laugh. "He's just ... eccentric." *Also, gorgeous. And talented.*

"Morgan's into bad boys. So, you never really had a chance."

"We should go in," Emerys said softly, disrupting the conversation.

Apparently romantic entanglements weren't high on her list of topics for discussion. Still, clearing that particular hurdle with Gethin left me feeling freer as we pushed open the gates and stepped onto hallowed ground.

The unease that had hit me before lingered, although less pronounced. Most of the headstones in the first few rows were in good order. I could see that someone had tended the grounds, clearing away old flowers and bits of detritus left behind by people paying their respect. I checked the dates on the nearest grave. Lucy Vincent had died at age forty-six two years ago. This was still a functioning cemetery.

As I looked out at the rows of graves, I noticed the grid like pattern of the layout. Each row had only ten plots in it. "Let me see that photo again."

Emerys passed it to me, and I studied the two numbers at the bottom of the address: 17. E5. "He's given us coordinates."

I looked up at the sky, trying to get a sense of the position of the sun and determine east and west. It was still low in the sky overhead. "This way." I headed to the far end of the first row and counted back five stones. Then, careful as I could, I walked forward seventeen rows. The headstone in front of me was for a Marjorie LeBlanc who died in 1985. But that didn't feel right.

"He probably wrote this down around when this photo was taken. So, what if we're starting at the wrong end?"

I didn't give my companions time to answer. Instead, I took off at a brisk walk until I made it to the very back of the grounds. The headstones in this section were in disrepair, many with barely legible dates and names. From my new starting position, I walked row by row, counting off to seventeen in my head. I stopped when I got there. We were maybe seven or eight rows back from Marjorie's grave. The dates on the markers around me were all from during the 1940s. I took a half-step back and looked down at the stones immediately to my left and right. The one on the right was for someone named Franklin Shaw, but the one to my left was for Wendell D. Byrne. The epitaph read: *Beloved Brother. On the road to Jericho, he sacrificed for King and Country. Honor et Praesidium aeternum.*

He'd died in 1944.

It seemed Wendell hadn't survived the Blitz after all. But why would Gaius have brought us to his brother's grave? Surely, he wouldn't have buried the Grail with him. Would he?

Beside me, Emerys tried and failed to hide the tears trickling down her cheeks as she took in the headstone before us. I reached out for her hand and gave it a soft squeeze, letting her know I understood her loss without words.

The longer I looked at the epitaph, the more something felt out of place. The phrase 'road to Jericho' tickled the back of my mind. "Jules, I've seen this before."

"Yeah, it's from the Bible. That's where the story of the Good Samaritan took place," she answered immediately. She'd grown up attending regular Sunday services.

Organized religion had never been top of Aunt Nim's priorities.

"That's right." But there was more to it. I crouched down, trailing my finger along each word. The metal on my left wrist grew warm and my fingertip left pale blue smudges on the gravestone, illuminating the words 'Brother' and 'Jericho.' "Fuck, I'm an idiot! It's right here in front of us."

Gaius hadn't gained the attention of some generous missionary who'd graciously reunited him with his brother. No, Wendell *was* Brother Jericho. He'd left this confirmation for us to find. He must have left the motto from the royal crest as a reminder, too. But it still didn't explain why he brought us here.

I closed my eyes, trying not to let the frustration building in the back of my mind overwhelm me. An image of a swatch of bright colors flashed through my mind, followed by shelves of books.

I'd seen them in the Crystal Cave when we'd first started this journey and I'd nearly forgotten all about them. But what did they mean?

Come on, magic, give me a sign.

'Seek me where things ancient find new life, where darker magic dwells.'

Gaius' voice echoed in my head and the image in my mind's eye grew sharper for the briefest of moments. The swirl of colors coalesced into a sign with a silver dragon logo.

"Where things ancient find new life, where darker magic dwells ..." I muttered under my breath.

"What was that?" Gethin asked.

"Ancient things that find new life," Jules repeated. "Sounds like antiques."

Where darker magic dwells ... well, shit. There was only one magical antiques market I knew of. And it was owned by my ex-boyfriend.

CHAPTER
SEVENTEEN

"No way," Jules protested once I'd explained my suspicion of where we were meant to go. "Morgan, you swore you'd never talk to him again."

"Why do I get the feeling I'm not going to like whoever you're talking about?" Gethin sighed.

"Because you won't," I replied. "Vance Langham is involved in the magical antiquities scene. And I'm getting the sense that's where we're meant to be going."

"Okay, and you can't talk to him, because ..."

"Because he's my ex and I turned him in to the magical police for trying to fence stolen magical artifacts."

Gethin's jaw went slack. "I don't want to offend

you, but that is far more interesting than the history I'd made up in my head."

"He's the reason Jules says I'm into bad boys. The minute I caught wind of what he was doing, I called the police."

"You said you'd never been arrested," Gethin noted.

"And until last night that was true. I reported him before he could rope me into anything illegal."

"And you think he'll be able to help us find Gaius and the Grail now?"

"He makes it his business to know all the other players on the scene."

"Perhaps before we approach him, we should attempt to find Gaius on our own?" Emery suggested.

"Believe me, I would love to never have to darken his door again. But as all of you keep reminding me, we're not the only ones searching for the Grail. We don't have the luxury of trying to sort this out ourselves or the time."

"You said you sort of heard Gaius' voice in your head, right?" Jules said.

"Yeah. I heard him at the abbey, too."

"What if there was another clue here, something we aren't seeing?"

"Like what?"

"We confirmed that his brother was actually Brother Jericho, right?"

"Yeah."

"And the slip of paper, well it kind of looks like a receipt. It mentions spirits. What if that was to make sure we found the grave?" Jules continued.

"The date!" I exclaimed. "Wendell died in 1944. Maybe it's the date we're meant to look into, the 25th of November 1944." I could feel my mood brightening. Maybe we didn't need Vance after all. "We just need to pay the local archives a visit and see what businesses were incorporated on that date."

"We still don't know what name he was going by then," Gethin pointed out.

"No, but we know the name he buried his brother under. I have to believe all those years later, he would have been comfortable going back to his own name. And there can't be that many businesses."

THERE WERE MORE than sixty businesses incorporated in and around the 25th of November 1944. Most looked to be related to the war effort. Nothing stood out to me as something that would be secreting the Holy Grail or even screamed antiques. And there wasn't anything I could find under Gaius' name, or anything referencing Jericho.

"I think I was wrong. You are going to have to pay him a visit," Jules sighed as we left the archives office.

We hadn't spoken in nearly three years. Vance used to be a regular at the Witching Hour, but since I'd turned him in, he'd stopped frequenting the bar. He used to maintain a shop not far from the bar, but again, I'd assumed the police had shut him down. There was one person who might know where to find him though.

"We're going to need to talk to Dean," I said. Jules gave me a sour look. "He is the only person I can think of who might know where Vance is these days."

Besides, a part of me felt bad having just abandoned my job tending bar. I owed it to the owners to at least give an explanation, even if they didn't need the whole story.

Usually bars weren't open this early, but today was inventory day. I'd typically worked a few overtime hours getting supplies back in stock and tracking everything. The bar was quiet when we walked in. It always amazed me how different it looked during the day with the lights on. The cool ambiance faded some in daylight.

"We're not open," Dean's voice echoed in the empty space.

"It's Morgan," I replied.

Dean's head popped up from behind the bar. He gave me a withering look. "Look who finally shows back up. You're lucky you bring in good tips. If I had my way, you'd have been fired after not showing up for weeks."

"My aunt died suddenly," I said sharply.

"Oh."

"Sorry my grief was inconvenient. But I was coming to tender my resignation anyway. I am leaving London."

I caught the look of surprise on Julayne's face out of the corner of my eye. I hadn't intended to come and hand in my notice, but it felt like the reasonable thing to do. If I was meant to make Camelot my home, it didn't make sense to keep a job I couldn't reasonably maintain or ghost my employer.

Dean looked uncomfortable as he processed the information. "Well, sorry for your loss. But you'll have to write out a formal notice you're quitting."

"Give me something to write on. I'll do it right now."

He rummaged behind the bar, producing a slip of receipt paper and a pen. It would have to do. I scribbled a note, tendering my resignation and signed my name and dated it. "Make sure this gets delivered."

"Yeah. Sure."

"You did want to ask that other thing," Jules whispered.

"Uh, right." I cleared my throat. "Are you still in touch with Vance?"

Dean let out a snort. "Looking for a goodbye shag before you go?"

"What I want with him is none of your business. Do you know where I can find him or not?"

"I might. But I'm pretty sure he won't talk to you."

"Did you not just hear her say it's her business? She doesn't need your bloody blessing," Jules spat.

"He's got a new shop on the edge of Greenwich Market, Red Roof Antiques."

"Thank you."

"You'd think he'd have learned his lesson the last time," Jules noted once we were back on the street.

I didn't disagree. Luckily, we weren't too far from the market. Still, I held my hand out to Jules. "Let me just check he's telling us the truth."

She passed me her phone and I looked up Red Roof Antiques. It had a rudimentary website, but I spotted Vance's name under the information about the owner. For once, Dean wasn't a complete dickwad.

The entire walk there, I played out the potential scenarios in my head of how this meeting might go. He could flat out refuse to even open the door. He could call the police on us and accuse me of harassing him. And those were the simple mundane options. He wasn't showy with his magic, but he was powerful in his own right. He could do serious damage when and if he wanted to.

Twenty minutes later, we stood in front of his shop. I scanned the awning, hoping maybe it sported a silver dragon. Alas, it was just a simple red fabric with the business name on it. I tried to take a step toward the door, but I froze in place.

"I could go in and see if he'd talk to me," Gethin offered. "He doesn't know me, and he wouldn't know I'm connected to you."

"Thanks, but I need to be the one to do this," I answered.

Shaking off my nerves, I reached for the door, but it swung inward before I could touch it. Vance stood on the other side of the threshold looking unsurprised to find me there.

"As I live and breathe. Morgan le Fey," he said.

"Hey, Vance. Been a while."

"Three years, four months and five days, but who's counting."

"Him apparently," Jules grumbled.

"I know you have no reason to even talk to me after everything between us. But we need help and you're the only person I could think of who might be able to find what we're after."

"And what are you after?"

"The Holy Grail," I replied.

"I'll bite. Come on in."

The shop was small, but not cramped. The items were clearly displayed to lead browsers deeper inside. I was no antiques expert, but even I could see the items closest to the window were far less expensive. He'd always had a good eye for design.

"You know, I got out of the game," he called as he rounded a desk at the back of the shop.

"Surprised you could get a license for all this after going away," Jules commented.

"Nice to see you too, Julayne." She glowered at

him and he smirked back. "I recognized the error of my ways before it came to any nasty business like prison. Those delightful blokes you sent after me realized I was a far better resource on the outside."

"So, you turned into a snitch," Jules snorted.

"I prefer the term informant," he said.

"Well, then it's a good thing we're looking for information," I said. "We think we know someone who might have a line on the Grail. Only problem is we're not sure where to find them. Just kinda pointed in the direction of your old stomping grounds."

He gestured to Gethin and Emerys. "I might be willing to help out some old friends, but I don't know them."

"This is Gethin. He's our mate. This is Emerys, she's a long-lost relative of mine."

"I'm going to need more than that," Vance replied.

"You need nothing more than Morgan's word," Emerys said sternly. I could feel power crackle around her.

"I don't trust people I don't know," he replied.

"Those stories my aunt used to tell me about Camelot were true," I blurted.

Vance hadn't been a real believer. Not like Jules.

But it had been a piece of my history I'd chosen to share with him. Without thinking, I pressed my index finger to the sapphire on the bracelet on my wrist. Excalibur sprang to life. It was a risk showing him the sword, but I trusted its magic wouldn't betray me.

His eyes lit up and I watched his fingers twitch. I shook my head. "You better believe you are talking to a princess. So, are you going to help us?"

"Yeah, all right. No need to get snippy."

I allowed Excalibur to return to its concealed form, keeping my gaze locked on Vance's face. "The person we're looking for would have established their business in 1944."

"And you think it's still in business today?"

"Yes."

"Well, there aren't too many old timers still around. And honestly, some of the ones left got swept up thanks to my contributions to the Crown's case."

"The owner might look younger than he really is."

"Or he might be the son of the original owner," Gethin suggested.

Vance didn't need to know we were hunting for a dragon.

The image of the silver dragon flashed through my mind again. "Maybe not an antiques dealer exactly. Rare books maybe? The awning has a silver dragon on it. Lots of colors behind it, a rainbow."

Vance's brow furrowed as he reached beneath the counter to retrieve a tablet computer. He tapped the screen a few times before rotating it so I could see. "Something like this?'

I took the device and zoomed in on the logo. I could now make out the words 'Est. 1944' beneath the curve of the dragon's body. "That's it."

"Draconis Rarities and Antiques," Vance said.

How had we missed that? It was right there in the name, screaming at us to find it. I scrolled down the page to find the address was located within Greenwich Market. But it was listed as by appointment only.

"You're not going to get in there. Not without an invitation and the bloke who runs it now is a bloody recluse."

"Let me worry about getting in," I said.

"Now hold on, I might know a way to grease the wheels. See, I've been trying to get in touch with the bloke about a couple of rare manuscripts. For a friend who is looking to acquire them."

I doubted there was anything friendly about

whomever he was working for. "And what, you think we can just pick them up for you on our way?"

"If you say I've sent you, it might be enough to get you in the door."

"You're really willing to risk your reputation to help me?"

"I was angry at you for turning me in for a long time, Morgan. But I see now how it's been to my benefit. Consider it a belated thank you."

The bell above the door let out a soft tinkling sound as someone walked in. I turned to find the three Seelie soldiers from the abbey filling up the tiny space.

"I thought we got rid of these arseholes," I groaned.

"It wasn't me this time," Gethin said.

"You should learn to conceal yourself better, Princess," the middle soldier said, tendrils of lightning crackling around his clenched fist.

"Whatever this is … take it the hell out of my shop," Vance ordered.

Unfortunately, the Seelies didn't appear inclined to acquiesce. The one with the lightning hands raised his fists, sending a blast hurtling straight for my face. I threw myself to the ground, dragging Jules and Gethin down with me. Emerys managed to throw up a defensive barrier, forcing the energy to dissipate on contact.

I saw one of the soldiers advancing around the perimeter of the room toward where the tablet lay. As quickly as I could, I deleted the search and shoved the device back at Vance. "Go!"

"You're insane if you think I'm letting some thugs wreck my shop," he replied and leapt over the counter. For a brief moment, I recalled all the times I'd thought of him as a badass. He tried to land a blow to the nearest soldier's torso, but found himself flung back against the counter, wheezing from the impact.

"You want to rethink that whole captain goes down with the ship bit?" I called.

"Not a bloody chance."

In that moment, all hell broke loose.

EIGHTEEN

Emerys raised her hands and I felt pulses of magic ripple outward from where she stood, trying to cut off their attacks. The soldier nearest to us began slamming his fists into the barrier, while his comrades flanked him. I watched in wordless horror as their barrage began to warp the wooden flooring, twisting to disrupt the spell.

"We need to get out of here," Jules called.

"And go where?" I retorted.

"We know the name of his shop and where it is. We just need to get out of here and make a break for it."

"You're insane if you think you're getting past those freaks," Vance said from behind the counter.

He'd lifted the partition that kept him and his customers separated.

I shoved Gethin ahead of me and pulled Jules behind me. "Emerys, let's go!"

She looked determined to hold the line, but as the wood continued to undulate at her feet, she scurried back to the protection of the counter. It wouldn't hold them for long. But it might give us enough time to regroup and come up with a better plan.

"Mind telling me who these guys are?" Vance asked as he twisted his hands in concentric circles, forming an energy sphere that he lobbed overhand at them. I heard one of them let out a hiss of pain from where Vance's magic had made contact.

"Oh, just mercenaries trying to kill me and steal what I'm after," I answered.

"We haven't talked for three years and suddenly your life gets interesting," he joked.

"They murdered Aunt Nim," I said darkly.

"Shit. I'm sorry."

"Maybe reconnect later. When we aren't about to be killed," Jules shouted as she jumped up, generating wind funnels that disrupted the nearest soldier's attempt to demolish the floor.

They weren't the only ones who could use the

environment around them to their advantage. I spotted an antique rocking chair near the front of the shop. I focused on it, picturing it rising from the floor to ensnare the nearest assailant. I felt Excalibur lending its magic to mine as I poured out my intent in the world. To my surprise, the chair rose off its rockers and did as I intended. It squeezed tight around the man's thick biceps and torso.

"Turn it back on them," I called to Emerys and pointed to the floor.

She flashed me a mischievous grin. With a wave of her hand, the floorboards that had already been warped, shot up into the air, forming into a vertical barrier that replicated itself whenever one of the Seelies touched it.

"We're still not leaving that way," Gethin pointed out as he rolled a few tiny balls out from beneath the counter. I watched as they erupted into little vines, rooting themselves in the exposed subflooring before trying to climb vigorously up the central Seelie's legs.

I turned my attention to Gethin's little defense plants, urging them to grow faster—with thorns— to keep them at bay. Unfortunately, the Seelie who'd been flanking from the left lobbed a series of fire balls at his compatriot in an effort to burn the plants away. They caught the exposed wood and surrounding antiques on fire instead. Smoke billowed into the air in thick grey clouds. I choked on the acrid fumes and threw myself to the ground, hoping Gethin and Emerys knew that smoke rises.

Thankfully, they stayed low, too. I had to wrangle Jules to keep her from trying to lob more magic over the counter at them. We didn't need the risk of them returning fire and blindly hitting their target through the smoke. Given the poor visibility, I couldn't risk creating another portal either. I'd barely managed the last one on my own and that was under better circumstances. I was beginning to see why Emerys didn't use it all the time. It really was a power drain. I didn't have time to feel guilty about giving her shit before. Guilt wasn't going to get us out of this situation.

If I could give us some reprieve from the smoke and flames, maybe we could get out of here. I made an expanding motion with my hands, giving it every ounce of magic I could, to clear the air of smoke and ash around us. I wasn't sure how long I could sustain it, but it was a start.

"You're really after the Holy Grail?" Vance coughed.

"Yeah. And to say it can't fall into their hands is

an understatement. If I had time, I'd explain every-thing that's happened. But just know, us having it is better for everyone."

"I lied before," he confessed. "I don't have any deals with the owner of Draconis. But he's a fucking legend. If he actually does talk to you, maybe put in a good word for me?"

"Help us get out of here and I'll think about it," I answered.

"So, I may have bought this place off an old bootlegger," he explained, starting to creep toward the back of the shop.

We had no choice but to follow after him. I did an awkward crouching walk to keep the bubble of clean air around the five of us. "And how is that useful?"

"Turns out, hiding your illegal alcohol from the local constabulary is a benefit to staying in business."

The air back here wasn't as rancid, and I let the magic fall away. I straightened. My legs complained at the sudden shift in my weight. I gritted my teeth to keep from swearing at the cramps in both of my calves.

Vance had led us into a office that looked unas-suming and mundane; until he pressed on a panel that swung inward to reveal a darkened passageway. I didn't like the idea of stepping through it. Not when I had no idea what might be waiting on the other side.

"It should lead you to street level in the market proper," he explained.

"Should?" I arched a skeptical brow at him.

"I haven't exactly had the chance to explore it," he replied. "As far as I know it's just a straight shot."

The smoke began to filter in from the front of the shop and the heat of the flames washed over me. For all I knew, the Seelies had abandoned their efforts, hoping we'd all burn to death.

"I don't like this. It feels too uncertain," Gethin said.

"I agree with him," Jules added.

"I know I have been a dick and I don't deserve to be seen as a decent human being, but I am literally trying to save your lives right now," Vance said, coughing into his sleeve.

"It would seem we have no choice. Either we turn back and fight and hope we are victorious, or we retreat and live to see another day. And perhaps find our intended destinies," Emerys said.

"You should come with us," I said before

thinking the words through. "No reason you need to stay in a literal burning building."

"This isn't my journey, Morgan. It's yours. And you've got people who have your back. I'm not going anywhere. These fuckers can try and take me down, but I'll be taking them down with me."

I hated that I'd put him in this position. I had never wanted to hurt him, even when I'd turned him in years ago. I'd been trying to prevent him from getting into worse trouble and falling in even deeper with dangerous magic wielders. But I could see the determination in his gaze. Vance wasn't going anywhere.

If he was willing to put his life on the line for me after everything we'd been through, then I could take him at his word that this tunnel would provide us an escape to where we needed to be.

"Thank you. I mean it," I said and leaned in to give him a quick peck on the cheek.

"Just go be a fucking hero, okay?" He looked at Jules. "Keep her safe."

"I always do," Jules retorted.

I'D NEVER BEEN HAPPIER to know Vance still had some less-than-legitimate connections than I was in that moment. Part of me felt bad leaving him behind to fend off the Seelie soldiers on his own. But he'd given us the information I needed, a way to get to Gaius. I just had to hope he hadn't succumbed so much to his reclusiveness as to not recognize me.

We followed the dead end tunnel until it stopped at a ladder leading up to street level. I climbed up first, trying to pry the cover free. "It's stuck," I called down.

Jules shimmied up the ladder after me, curling her body around me to try and leverage the other side of the cover. "On three," she said.

"One. Two. Three!"

We both pushed at the same time and managed to dislodge the cover, sliding it along the pavement. Sunlight filled the darkened tunnel. I eased myself up to sit on the edge of the hole, peering around to make sure we hadn't been followed via the street level. From what I could tell, we were alone.

I maneuvered myself to pull Jules out, then Gethin and Emerys. I took in the marketplace, hoping we didn't have far to go to find Gaius' shop. In the distance, I could hear what sounded suspiciously like explosions. My pulse quickened in my neck, starting to distort my hearing and vision. I couldn't help but picture Vance injured in his shop, actually sacrificing his life so I could get away. Hot tears pricked the back of my eyes at the imagined prospect of yet another person I'd known losing their life all because of me. In that moment, doubt screamed in my head. How was I supposed to be a leader when I couldn't even keep the people I cared about safe? I'd lost Aunt Nim. Was I even actually worthy of the power Excalibur bestowed on me? Or was I just lucky enough to have the right blood in my veins to wield it?

"Where are we going, Morgan?" Jules urged, pulling me out of my mental spiral.

I swallowed the lump rising in my throat and dried my eyes. I wiped some of the ash and soot from my face as I took a steadying breath. This wasn't the time to wallow or feel sorry for myself at the shit life had thrown at me recently. Not when we're so close to achieving what we'd set out to do. I scanned the nearby awnings before turning back to orient myself with the entrance of the market. The curved metal sign of the market stood behind us. Okay, that meant we needed to go deeper.

The compass beneath my shirt grew warm and I pulled the chain free. It cast ethereal footprints on the ground, leading away from where we stood. It had gotten me this far, maybe it would take us all the way. I took off at a brisk jog until we'd passed half a dozen shops and stalls. There, at the far end of the market stood a little shop with a multi-colored banner featuring a silver dragon. "There!"

I took off at a sprint now, skidding to a halt at the front door. I couldn't see much through the window, but I thought I heard movement from within. Maybe my mind was playing tricks on me. Either way, I was going inside. I turned the handle on the door to find it locked. Apparently, Gaius was serious about his no walk-ins policy. I'd have to brute force my way in. I closed my eyes, picturing the lock releasing, the tumblers falling into place to undo the bolt and I heard a soft click. When I tried the handle again, it twisted in my grip, and I eased it inward. A bell above the door announced my entry.

I gestured for the others to hang back. There was no need for all of us to get into a scuffle if this somehow went sideways. I had to believe he could be rather annoyed I'd just broken into his shop, even if he had led me there via his trail of clues. Besides, Gaius had only met me once before. I didn't need to make him uneasy with unfamiliar faces or unexpected blasts from the past.

"Hello?" I called. "Gaius?"

I could definitely hear movement from the back of the shop, but no one responded. I glanced over my shoulder, hoping my friends had a suggestion. Jules mimed taking something from my pocket and mouthed, 'paper.'

Of course, the paper that had been written out like some kind of receipt. I understood now why it said remit to holder. He needed to know I was the right person to give the Grail to. Even if someone had found the receipt and photograph at the abbey, if they didn't know our history, the clues might not have made sense.

"Hello? I'm looking for the proprietor," I tried again. "I have a receipt for an item that I need to pick up. It's rather urgent."

"I don't have any appointments today," a tired voice answered. It sounded like Gaius if a bit older.

He stared at me, as if he was waiting to see what I would do next. "... I think we made an appointment a long time ago," I finally answered.

He came out from the back of the shop and I caught the look of recognition in his eyes. But they clouded over with unease and he shook his head, as if he doubted my identity.

I would give him the benefit of the doubt,

because it had been several centuries from his perspective since last we spoke. Still, he gestured for me to step further into the shop.

I stepped up to the counter that separated us and set the slip of paper on the surface. At this distance I could see that he wore a simple button-down shirt with the sleeves rolled up to his elbows and trousers secured with a simple leather belt low around his hips. I wouldn't have thought anything of him just passing one another on the street. It might have been centuries since he'd seen me, but I could still picture him in his simple tunic from the Tower. I tapped the first line of the receipt. "Jericho spirits, 25 November. The date you established this shop." I laid the photograph of him and his brother on the counter.

He didn't say anything, but he didn't turn me away either. I caught him subtly tracing the edge of the photograph where Wendell stood, proudly displaying his medic's uniform. At least he recognized it.

"Wares of kings," I continued, pointing to the second item on the receipt. "That would be the item I am looking for. Its value to both of us is priceless, I believe. You gave up a lot to keep it safe."

"And what say you, if I should ask by what right you believe you have claim to any of my wares?"

Please let this be the right answer. "*Honor et Praesidium aeternum,*" I said, praying I hadn't butchered the pronunciation.

"*Materna magica,*" he answered.

Camelot's royal motto.

The doubt faded from his features and his lips parted into a broad, toothy grin. It made him look decades younger and more like the man I'd encountered in the Tower. He let out a sigh that turned into a joyous laugh. "I have been waiting a very long time for you, Morgan Pendragon."

NINETEEN

I stared at the man behind the counter in the cramped bookshop as he continued to shake with laughter. His hair had greyed some. Only it was more a salt and pepper look than anything betraying his age—at the very least hundreds of years old.

"You remember me?" Gethin, Emerys and Jules crowded into the shop behind me.

"It is difficult to forget the young woman who walked into my prison cell all those centuries ago, brandishing my liege's family blade." He turned and gave Emerys a deep bow. "Your Highness."

"I have not gone by that title in a very long time, old friend," she said and approached him.

"You may no longer be Camelot's Queen, but you will always be mine." He stepped out from behind the counter and allowed her to embrace him in a firm hug.

I watched as they held tight to one another. "We mourned you," she finally said.

"Wendell and I knew we would never return to the halls of Camelot. It was better we give those we left behind some closure."

"It nearly broke him to leave you both behind."

"It was not such an easy thing for us either, to stay in a realm so unfamiliar. But it was made easier knowing you hailed from these lands." He gave her a soft smile. "He told us of your visits. For a time, I had hoped we might cross paths, but it was not to be. Not until now."

"Visits?" I interrupted.

Emerys released her grip on Gaius and turned back to me. "In the years after I left this realm, I would venture back through the barrier. Just far enough to feel this world's magic again. For a time, I reconnected with my kin here too." She glanced back at Gaius. "If I had known the truth, I would have sought you out."

"We were sorry to hear about your brother's death," I added.

"Dragons may be long-lived, but we are not invincible. He died doing what he loved. He was trying to protect a group of children when bombs fell."

"Not to rush the reunion," Jules said, "But we still have Seelie thugs after us and the Grail."

"Do not worry, young lady, I may be an old dragon, but even I remember what Seelie magic feels like. I have wards in place to keep them out."

"These blokes are relentless," I said. "They murdered my aunt and have been trying to kill me ever since."

"That you are standing here, relatively unharmed, shows that you carry Malachi's determination in your veins."

"That she does," Emerys agreed.

Without warning, the walls of the shop shook. Waves of energy cascaded from the ceiling to the floorboards. I didn't need to ask to know those were the anti-Seelie wards he'd mentioned a few moments ago. They'd found us. While I didn't disbelieve him that his magic was strong enough to keep them out, I didn't want to test the wards' limits.

"Jules is right. We came for the Grail. It's time for it to return home to Camelot."

He looked from me to Jules and back again. "Yes, I believe it is. Both of you come with me."

"We'll try to hold them off if they get through," Gethin said, turning to face the front door.

Jules and I followed Gaius back into the depths of the shop. The shelves of neatly organized books gave way to a workroom of sorts. I could see old books laid out with materials for restoring the bindings and ensuring that the leather covers didn't crack. It appeared after all these years, he'd found something that suited him. Still, I saw the wistful expression on his face as he reminisced with Emerys about their past.

He bent down to a low cabinet made of ornate cherry wood and his fingers shifted, his nails becoming talons and his skin rippling into scales. He pressed his transformed hand against the front of the cabinet, and it gave a soft hiss as a hidden compartment opened. He reached in and retrieved something in a small velvet pouch.

Beyond the room where we stood, I could hear the sounds of walls shaking and I thought I even picked up on the cracking of structural supports. We had to hope Gaius' protective magic extended to the literal brick and mortar in the building. Otherwise, we might end up buried in rubble.

When Gaius stood, he pivoted to face us, but his attention fell squarely on Julayne. He tugged the bag down to reveal the chalice I'd seen in my vision from the Crystal Cave. Despite the dim lighting, the object glowed with a vibrant amber shimmer. Upon closer inspection, what I'd assumed to be gold before was in fact tiny shards of amber embedded in the metal, Surrounding the larger gem at the chalice's center.

"You trust this woman with your life, young Pendragon?"

"Of course, I do," I answered.

"And you have shared the journey to retrieve this blessed vessel?"

"I couldn't have done it without Jules. I truly believe she was meant to be in this whole thing with me. She's my best friend. We're like sisters."

He accepted my answers and held the chalice out for Julayne to take. "If you are truly worthy, the Grail will know."

She glanced back at me. "Here goes everything."

She took the Grail in both hands, and her face reflected in the gemstone at its center. When she turned, I could see the gem's amber reflection in her pupils, as if she was somehow connected to the chalice.

Another concussive boom rocked the shop walls around us. Somewhere beyond us, alarms began to blare. Water shot out from overhead sprinklers, threatening the stacks of antique books in the shop proper.

Julayne's eyes returned to their normal blue and her shoulders sagged. "It accepted me."

"Great. Now how do we stop these lunatics from burning the place to the ground with us inside?"

"Uh, you might want to hurry up back there!" Gethin shouted. "They've breached the wards!"

I looked at Gaius. "I thought you said they'd hold?"

"Perhaps I overestimated my magic's strength. I fear my power is fading as of late. That my time to walk this world may soon end. And if that is so, I will meet my fate as a knight ought to. On the field of battle." His other hand shifted into scales and talons. His eyes took on an orange tinge around his irises.

Jules stowed the Grail in her bag and secured it across her torso before leading the charge back into the shop proper. The water sputtering down overhead was enough to keep things from catching fire, but I could still smell smoke from the Seelie soldiers' attempts to break through the wards and the building's foundation.

I held tight to the sapphire at the heart of the

bracelet, pouring as much power into it as I could. Excalibur leapt to attention, shifting back to its rightful form in a heartbeat. One of the soldiers, who I hadn't had the pleasure of tussling with yet, lunged for me with both hands outstretched. I was about to try and block him with Excalibur's hilt when Gaius appeared, and his talons dug deep into the soldier's forearms. The dragon sent the Seelie hurtling into the nearest bookshelf, sending priceless tomes tumbling onto the wet ground.

That left the four of us to take on the two remaining soldiers. One lobbed a fireball at Emerys, and she deflected it, sending it colliding with some more of Gaius' books. The aged pages and soft leather caught fire and burned almost instantly. I watched as Gethin did his best to redirect the sprinkler flow to the pile of burning paper.

"The books don't matter," Gaius called. "Protect Morgan. She is what is important!"

The same Seelie who'd just attacked Emerys turned his sights my direction. He sent jets of flame at me, and I raised Excalibur, intending to deflect the blows as best I could into the already wet flooring. Instead, Excalibur's blade turned a blinding white as it absorbed the magic. I could feel the power course through my body, as if someone had hooked me up to a car battery.

"I've had just about enough of you lot trying to hurt my friends," I shouted, my voice somehow amplified in the space.

Jules stepped up beside me and we clasped hands. The energy I felt crackling along every nerve ending leapt to Jules and I could see her aura flare with the same golden shimmer as the Grail.

Everything moved in slow motion as we moved as one entity with a singular purpose. We moved in lock step as beams of magic shot out from our joined hands, colliding with one opponent and then the next. All of the Seelie soldiers vanished from the shop. The walls shook, but this time from our power. In my mind, I'd put out into the world that I wanted to protect this place and its inhabitants. Somehow, I knew Jules had done the same.

When she finally dropped my hand, Jules' body slumped. Gethin was by her side to catch her before she fell. I looked to see Gaius still slumped against the bookshelves. His hands had reverted back to human form, and I could see the strain in his eyes to have sustained his partially shifted body for even that long. I offered him a hand up. He took it, steadying himself against the shelves as he did so.

The moment Excalibur returned to bracelet form on my wrist, I too felt the wave of exertion crash over me. It was Gaius' turn to offer me a supporting hand as he led me to the restoration room and to a chair. Gethin helped Jules as Emerys brought up the rear. Alarms continued blaring and the sprinklers still splattered the shop with their half-hearted attempts to put out the flames.

To my surprise no emergency personnel—mundane or magical—had arrived to check out the commotion. Had Gaius' wards kept those types of people out, too? The shopkeeper disappeared for a few minutes and upon his return, the blaring ceased.

"Sorry about the shop," I said, my voice worn out.

"As I said, you are far more important than these old books."

"But ... They're your treasures," I said, gesturing to the ones that had remained unharmed in here. "It's obvious you take great pride in your work. I don't have money, but I'll find a way to repay you somehow."

He waved away my offer. "Consider it this old knight's last duty to his crown. It was an honor to defend a Pendragon once more."

"Are you sure you won't come back with us?" I said, sitting up.

"It surprises me to admit, but this place, these people, have become my home." He gave a soft, contemplative laugh. "Those were words I never thought I would ever speak."

"You would be welcomed home a hero," Emerys added.

"I did what was asked of me, because it was the honorable and noble thing to do."

"Well, then perhaps we will cross paths again one day, old friend," she said.

"I do hope so."

"Morgan, you here?" Vance's voice came from the front of the shop.

"What's he doing here?" I heard the note of irritation in Julayne's voice.

I pushed myself to my feet and wound my way again to the front. He looked around at the state of the shop. "You've really got it out for antiques."

"What are you doing here?"

"I wanted to make sure you were okay. Those freaks left after you went through the passage. I thought they might have figured out where you'd come."

"How noble," Jules called from her seat in the back.

"We're fine. We got rid of them."

"Yes, where did you send them?" Gaius asked, eyeing Vance.

"Basement cells in the Tower of London," I answered with a smirk. It wouldn't keep them distracted for long, but they'd have some explaining to do when they were discovered.

Gaius grinned. "I approve." He gestured to Vance. "You look familiar. Why do you look familiar?'

"I'm Vance Langham, proprietor of Red Roof Antiques."

"The conspirator to the law," Gaius noted in a dismissive tone.

"I don't think he likes you," I said.

"Pity, I was sort of hoping he might be interested in a partnership. As it happens, my establishment has undergone a bit of ... unexpected remodeling and I'm in need of some temporary lodgings. And I see that some of your inventory has taken a rather unfortunate hit as well. We could help each other out."

"I really didn't mean for your place to catch fire,"

I said when Vance fixed me with a half-hearted glare.

"Perhaps we could come to an arrangement," Gaius said. "But I do not traffic misbegotten wares."

"Wouldn't dream of it. I promise, those days are behind me."

"A trial basis, I think. With the possibility of a more permanent arrangement in the future," Gaius called.

"Sounds perfect. I promise, you won't regret it."

"Don't make promises you can't keep young man."

Vance gave me a look that said, 'What's that about?'

I shrugged. I wasn't about to tell him his new business partner was a several-hundred-year-old dragon. "I can't believe I'm actually saying this, but thanks for the help today," I said to Vance as Gaius returned to the back room. "You actually came through. And honestly, I had my doubts."

"I haven't exactly given you reasons to think I'd be there for you," he said. "Look, I know we've had our differences, Morgan. But I want you to know, I'm around if you ever need help. I really have changed."

Part of me wanted to believe him. But the part

that had seen what he was capable of wasn't ready to make that leap. "I'll keep it in mind."

I turned to my companions and said, "We'd better get back before they catch up to us again."

"Yes, I think it is about time we go home," Emerys agreed.

I held out my hand for Julayne. "You ready to have all of your wildest dreams come true, Jules?"

She grabbed my hand, using it to pull herself to her feet and flashed me a wide grin. "Let's go to freaking Camelot!"

TWENTY

I never would have guessed I'd be happy to be going back to the middle of nowhere Ireland. But I was practically giddy as we left the tourists behind and marched straight on toward the barrier that would lead us to Albion and back to Camelot. I looked over my shoulder at my travel companions and couldn't hide the sense of contentment that filled me from head to toe.

I had thought I'd lost all of my family the day my Aunt Nim died, but I was wrong. It had always been there, with how Jules supported me even when I didn't believe in myself. Also, in the way Emerys never gave up looking for me. The fact she'd prolonged her own life just to meet me and guide me. I never thought anyone would have been willing to take such steps for me.

Julayne fell into step beside me, shifting the bag over her shoulder that now housed the Holy Grail. "You seem happier," she noted.

"I feel happier. Saying it out loud sounds a bit childish I suppose, but I never realized just how much I needed you doing this with me."

"You and I both know we're a package deal." After a moment she added, "I think Nim must have sensed something to have trusted me so much with all of the stories about Camelot. She knew I'd help keep you on track in meeting your destiny."

There were still so many questions I wished I could ask her. How much did she know about the quest for the Grail? Had she purposely set Jules on the path to help me track it down? But all of these questions I would never get the answer to since she was gone.

"So, what do you think we'll be walking back into when we get there?" Jules made a vague gesture at the empty air ahead of us.

"Honestly, I don't know. Things were tense when we left, but it didn't feel like fighting would pop off right away." Even still, I doubted if Shunae and her delegation had fixed things yet.

"Speaking of home, we should not waste any more time returning," Emerys called.

I led the way through the barrier. Unlike the first time I'd passed through, there was no sense of disorientation this time. It was like simply walking through a doorway from one room to another. Beside me, Jules faltered as her foot slid on some loose brush and rocks. I reached out and caught her with both hands.

"Sorry, should have warned you about the forest," I said.

Jules, having caught her balance, looked around. Her mouth hung open in awe as she took a slow spin. I watched as the awe turned into excitement. "I have so many questions. Like how've we got a field on the other side and yet here is a full-on forest?" She took a big inhale through her nose. "And does the air always smell this sweet?"

"We will have time enough to marvel over the many differences between this world and yours, but we must return to the castle posthaste. The Queen needs to know her heir has returned home safe," Emerys interjected.

"I'll give you the quick tour," Gethin told Jules, offering his arm.

She flashed me a grin before taking it and

allowing him to lead her off ahead of us. I fell into step beside Emerys as we made our way toward the lake and her cabin. We'd have to portal back into the castle, since we were meant to not have left it in the first place.

"I'm sorry you couldn't convince Gaius to return with us."

"This is not the world nor the life he left behind any longer," she said softly. "I could not ask him to abandon the ties he had made in your world."

"His magic was fading, though. Wouldn't returning to Albion have strengthened him?"

"Perhaps. But he has grown old, Morgan. He is ready to let his power fade and join his kin."

"Would you ever want to go back to where you came from?" I pressed.

"I have no living descendants any longer in that world. My lineage is here with your mother and with you. Any connection I held there passed centuries ago."

I glanced back over my shoulder at the woods as they receded. I couldn't imagine not wanting to go back, even just for a visit. Maybe that would change one day, when this place felt more like my home than London. But that day wasn't today.

We'd made it about halfway to the cabin when my head erupted in pain. I stumbled over my own feet, falling to my knees as I pressed my hands to my temples and squeezed my eyes shut. Images of the Crystal Cave flashed across my vision, somehow shining so vibrantly I feared I would go blind if I tried to open my eyes.

I felt hands on my back and leaned into their supportive touch. Another pair of hands wrapped tight around my wrist and tugged my hands away from my face. I was still too hesitant to open my eyes though.

"Morgan, talk to me." Julayne's voice was comforting, but firm.

"My head!" I managed as the cave's interior continued to flash in my mind.

Coolness danced along my skin and up to my temples where the pain eased. I recognized Julayne's magic at work and instantly relaxed. I cracked one eyelid and when I could still make out her facial features above me, I opened the other eye. The worry lines around her mouth were a bit fuzzy as my eyes adjusted to my surroundings again.

"I think I'm supposed to go back to the cave," I said once the pain fully subsided.

"Has this ever happened before?" Jules eased me to my feet, keeping a firm grip on my wrist.

"No. But it feels like the cave is calling to me," I answered.

"Can it do that?" This time Gethin's voice entered the mix, carrying a heavy weight of concern.

"I have not witnessed such a feat, but magic is potent there and Morgan holds a unique position in this realm. It appears she holds some unforeseen connection with the cave in particular," Emerys answered.

"Then we go to the cave," Jules said, and we turned back, the way we'd come.

The closer we got to the cave, the more I felt it pulling, urging me onward. It *needed* me and that scared me. I couldn't put into words why, but it felt ominous as I approached. I didn't want to enter alone. I kept a tight hold on Jules. However, the moment I set foot into the mouth of the cave, our physical connection vanished. In my peripheral vision I watched as she, Gethin, and Emerys went flying backward out of view.

I made a move to leave the cave, but found my feet were only capable of carrying me deeper inside until I found myself next to the small pool at the back of the space.

"My friends better not be hurt," I said, not feeling as foolish as I might have even a week ago.

"Your companions will be unharmed," my reflection answered. She stood in much the same position I did, except Excalibur sat strapped to her hip.

On instinct, my right hand brushed against my left wrist to find the metal still wound around it. Tension melted from between my shoulder blades. The sword wasn't the only difference between us. She held the Grail at her other side. But it looked different somehow.

"I found the Grail and brought it back to Camelot where it belongs," I said, gesturing to the chalice in my reflection's grasp. "So, what's with the summons that nearly blinded me?"

My reflection held up the chalice, inspecting it. "Retrieving this was not your only objective."

"I had to do it with Jules. I got that part, too," I answered.

"Earning her trust was not the whole of your task."

"Trust? She's been my mate for ages. Literally the only other person I've known longer was my Aunt Nim. Why wouldn't I trust Jules? I shouldn't have to earn her trust."

"She had to prove herself worthy of pledging to your cause," my reflection noted.

"She would have done that if I'd just asked, without a quest or whatever that was needed," I argued.

"The fight you face requires a deeper bond, one of magic and sacrifice to shield you from your enemies," my reflection noted cryptically.

That's as clear as mud. Talk in plain fucking words."

She held the amber chalice up, spinning it so the gem embedded in its center gleamed. "It isn't enough for her to have earned your trust or your friendship. To secure your bond, she must give you this, blessed by her own magic."

I watched as my reflection plucked the gem free of the metal and it glowed with a vibrant purple aura before it disappeared from sight. Why I needed the migraine and the cryptic clues to get this information, I didn't know. But it didn't matter. I had no doubt Jules would give me the gem and secure our bond.

"Once she's done that, what do we do with the Grail?"

"If you ever have need of healing from a mortal

wound, it will grant you reprieve from death … but only once."

"No eternal life or youth?" I quipped.

"We aren't meant to live forever," my reflection answered as the sword at her side and the chalice vanished. Whatever magic resided in the cave had passed on its message.

I stayed rooted to the rocky ground for a moment, half expecting something else to happen. Nothing did. I took a couple steps toward the mouth of the cave and found myself able to move freely. I hurried out of the cave back into the woods, casting about for my travel companions. I spotted Gethin first.

"Oi, mate … you, okay?" I called, shaking him by the bicep.

He let out a groan and reached his other hand up to his head. "Ow! What happened?"

"Uh, the cave wanted a private chat and got a bit aggressive about it," I replied and hauled him to his feet.

"Well, that wasn't very polite," he grumbled.

A quarter of a meter away, I saw Emerys pulling herself up from where she'd landed, too. She looked less disoriented than Gethin, but the annoyance on her face was clear even from this distance. That just left Julayne. She'd been standing right in front of the cave when we'd been forcibly separated. But I didn't see her anywhere.

"Jules?" I called. "Where are you?'

No answer.

I left Gethin's side, searching the underbrush for signs that Jules had gotten up already. I found some depressions in the leaves and low branches, but nothing obvious to tell me where she'd gone. Panic tightened my chest as I got farther from the cave. *Could the magic that had split us up really sent her this far?*

"Julayne!" My voice came out in a croak.

My heart hammered in my throat and my pulse pounded in my ears until I spotted a spray of dark hair ahead of me. *Oh, thank God.* I scurried up the small embankment, only momentarily noting just how close she'd come to landing beyond the barrier. She lay there on the ground, limbs fully splayed, and the bag concealing the Grail tossed off her shoulder by a nearby tree.

"Hey, come on, let's get you up," I said as I bent to shift her weight, so she rested against me.

She gave a soft moan and her eyes fluttered open. A look of momentary confusion melted away and she sat up straighter. "What happened?"

"Magic cave being a dickwad," I answered.

"How long was I out?"

"Not sure." I turned my gaze skyward. It didn't look like we'd been apart for more than maybe fifteen minutes. "Not long, I think."

I eased her to an upright position. Together we rejoined Emerys and Gethin who had mostly recovered themselves now. "I trust your journey within was illuminating?" Emerys noted.

The memory of the vibrancy of the cave's summons was enough to set my teeth on edge. "Maybe don't use that word. But yeah, it was important." I turned to Jules. "Apparently everything we've already been through isn't enough for the universe. We've got to be magically bonded, too."

"Why?" The unease in her voice surprised me.

"I'm learning not to question mystical signs," I replied. "It doesn't seem like it's going to be hard." I gestured to the bag. "You've got to ... I guess imbue some of your magic into the gem and uh, give it to me."

Jules opened the bag and took out the Grail. Her eyes widened as the sun glinted off the vibrant amber gem at the center. "Are you absolutely sure?"

"That cave led me back to you for a reason. I trust it," I said.

Jules pressed her fingers to the metal around the gem and heat sizzled, warping the connection between cup and gem until the latter fell free. Jules set the amber chalice down and cupped the gem in her hands. I could feel power radiating from her hands. I took a step forward, holding out my hands, too. The lime scent of my magic coated my skin in a thin greenish film as she passed the gem to me. Unlike the vision I'd seen in the cave, the gem didn't glow the same vibrant purple. Still, I could feel a hint of her magic winding around my own, like a lattice work to make us both stronger. The gem turned liquid, pouring over my skin, and forming into a thin band around my left middle finger.

I pulled her into a tight hug, grateful that this journey was done, for now. We left the forest behind and regrouped.

"Come on, let's get back to the castle. I've got so much to show you," I said and looped my arm through Jules'. We filed through Emerys' portal to Camelot.

As we turned to head down the hall, I saw a figure move just beyond the closing portal. The worry that washed over me faded along with the portal.

Whoever or whatever it was, they were far from the castle and for now, not a threat. I didn't know how long we had to enjoy just being together again in this new land, living out our childhood fantasy, but I would take it. War still loomed on the horizon if Camelot's delegation couldn't convince the Seelies to back down. But for the moment, I could almost forget about that danger.

QUICK AUTHOR'S NOTE

I AM NOT USUALLY a big discovery writer. I generally come into a book having a sense of what's going to happen. Not all the details are fleshed out but I feel like this book more than most was really a surprise on what came out as I wrote. Coming out of the high-action of book 1, this one felt a lot slower-paced and really focused on emotions and relation-ships. Did that mean there wasn't any action? Of course not. But to me, it felt like we needed to catch our breath after all the drama from Morgan coming back to Camelot and unearthing Arthur's betrayal.

I knew I wanted to showcase and really establish the connections Morgan is making with the other characters around her, especially with Gethin and Julayne. They are in a way, standing in for the Guinevere and Lancelot characters and so I needed to really show her links to both of them. I also knew I needed to not leave people in the dark about Morgan and Emery's connection. That is honestly something I struggle with as a writer. I get these ideas for little side stories or prequels and I'm terrible about weaving that information back into the mains tory. Intellectually I know not everyone reads the extras. I promise I'm working to address that writerly flaw!

But overall, I really enjoyed this book. It was a fun little quet to find the Holy Grail and it cements Julayne as Morgan's first knight. And we got to explore a little more lore from other magical cultures from Albion while also getting to see some sights in magical London. I had a lot of fun picking the places they'd end up visiting because I knew I didn't want to do the typical ones. Yes, they did visit the Tower of London, but beyond that, their journey took them to some more unusual places. I also loved finding ways to bring Nim back into the conversation. There is a lot I would love to do with her character through shorter content.

Morgan returns back to Camelot at the end of this story and while we haven't ended on a cliffhanger exactly, things aren't as they might appear. I know where Morgan's next quest takes her and I beyond thrilled to be following her there. You'll just have to wait and see where that is!

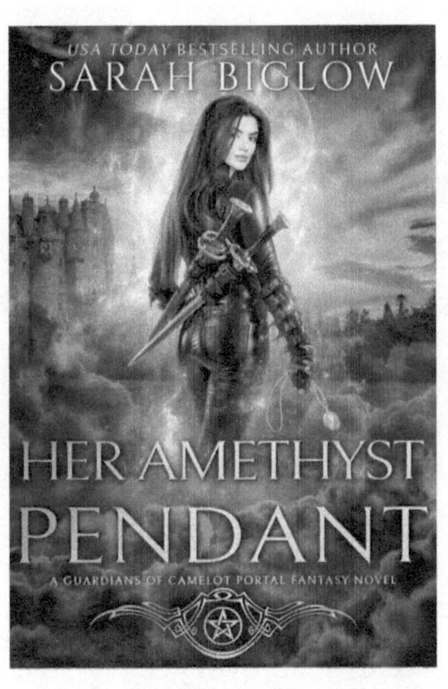

Her Amethyst Pendant

When peace falters, can she keep her kingdom safe?

Camelot is finally starting to feel like home for Morgan. She's bonded with the mother she never knew and her best friend is at her side in this fantastical new world. When a massive cyber attack on Camelot's defenses throws her people into chaos and leaves the tentative peace with the Seelies on the precipice of war, Morgan must heed the call of a new quest to find a much-needed ally.

Morgan's search leads her to the heart of Boston where she must track down a witch capable of protecting her kingdom and strengthening her sisterhood of knights. Finding her way in a city steeped in magic may be more than she bargained for. The roots of power run deep and the secrets she unearths about her own history may prove more dangerous than she realizes.

Even if she can convince this newfound companion to join the cause, not everything is as it appears. Returning home to Camelot may not be enough to stop the drums of war from sounding. Will Morgan be able to protect her people before its too late?

Scan the QR code to get your copy of Her Amethyst Pendant.

About the Author

Sarah Biglow is a *USA Today* bestselling author. She lives in Massachusetts with her husband and son. She is a licensed attorney and spends her days combatting employment discrimination as an Investigator with the Massachusetts Commission Against Discrimination.

You can find an up-to-date list of all my books here